HENRY TILNEY'S DIARY

HENRY TILNEY'S DIARY

Amanda Grange

ROBERT HALE · LONDON

ISBN 978-0-7090-9233-9

Robert Hale Limited
Clerkenwell House
Clerkenwell Green
London EC1R 0HT

www.halebooks.com

2 4 6 8 10 9 7 5 3 1

Typeset in 11/16pt Galliard
Printed and bound in Great Britain by
the MPG Books Group, Bodmin and King's Lynn

Dedicated to everyone at the Jane Austen House Museum, Chawton, Home of England's Jane. With many thanks for their excellent work and for making me so welcome.

1790

Wednesday 14 April

No lessons, no tutors, no Latin, no Greek! How glad I am to be home again, with time to spend with my horses and dogs, my brother and sister, my mother and father. No more school for a month! Instead time to wander the abbey and roam the grounds.

The kitchen gardens have changed since last I was here. My father took me on a tour of them as soon as I stepped out of the carriage. He would not be content until I had seen every new plant and marvelled over every new bit of walling. It gives him something to do, now that he has left the army, I suppose, and I believe he will change every part of the Abbey before he is done.

Mama looked pale but only laughed when I said so, remarking that everyone looks pale in April. But I think she is not well. Eleanor has grown another inch and has developed a taste for Gothic novels. Frederick was out all day and looks set to be out all night, too. Papa paced up and down, his watch in his hand, whilst waiting for my brother this evening, then at last gave instructions for dinner to be served without him. I do not envy Frederick when he returns, for if there is one thing my father hates, it is to be kept waiting for anything.

Thursday 15 April

All was peaceful this morning as Mama, Papa and I were at breakfast. Eleanor had just departed to work with her governess when suddenly the door of the breakfast parlour opened and Frederick walked in. It was obvious that he had just returned from a night's carousing. He was looking very dishevelled. His eyes were red, his speech slurred and his linen was none too fresh. He lurched towards us and demanded a thousand pounds from my father to cover his losses at the gaming tables, saying he must pay his debts of honour. My father, who had watched him like a simmering volcano since he set foot in the room, went purple with rage and rose to his feet. He shook with anger and then erupted, roaring a refusal and saying that Frederick had disgraced the name of Tilney.

'By God, boy! What do you mean by it, coming in here at this hour and standing before your mother in this state, unwashed and reeking of brandy? I have warned you about your behaviour before, sir, but I will not warn you again. I have had my fill! I will not stand by whilst you waste every penny of your allowance—'

'Aye, and pennies is all it is,' said Frederick with a sneer. 'A gentleman cannot be expected to manage on what you give him. It is a trifling sum, when you inherited a fortune—'

'Which you are dissipating. I should never have listened to your mother's soft entreaties on your behalf. I should have sent you into the army years ago, it would have made a man of you,' said my father.

'What? A soldier?' asked Frederick as he half-lurched, half-fell into a chair with a derisory laugh. 'I am the heir of Northanger Abbey. Careers are not for the likes of me.'

'Careers are for every man who would be a man, instead of a disgrace to himself, his family and his name. The devil finds work for idle hands; well, no more! If you were older I would demand your help in running the estate—'

Frederick snorted.

'You would never let me meddle with your precious gardens and kitchens, you want them all to yourself. You do not even let Mama have a say! You like your own way too well.'

Papa threw down his napkin and his anger turned into icy contempt.

'If you had shown any interest in your duty, then in the coming years I would have let you join with me in improving the abbey, but as it is you need discipline. Let us see what a few years in the army will do for you, and see if you, too, can rise to the rank of general.'

Mama, who had been sitting quietly up until that point, was upset by the turn events had taken. She implored my father to change his mind, saying that Frederick was too young to join the army. To which my father replied, 'Eighteen? Too young? If anything it is too old. Some discipline would have done the boy good years ago, but better late than never.' Then turning to Frederick he demanded, 'Well, sir, what do you have to say for yourself?'

Frederick looked mutinous, but Papa in one of his moods is not a man to cross, and so instead of challenging our father outright Frederick said provokingly, 'That I think it a very good thing.'

'Do you begad?' said my father in surprise. He nodded his approval. 'Then perhaps there is hope for you yet.'

But Frederick had not finished.

'There is nothing more calculated to attract the opposite sex than a red coat,' he said impudently. 'The women fall all over me at the moment, they will fall even more quickly once I am in uniform!'

My father was incensed.

'Puppy!' he roared.

'Please, dear, do reconsider,' Mama implored him. 'Frederick is the heir. He cannot go into the army. What will happen if he is killed?'

'He will be killed if he stays at home. He is forever putting his horse at breakneck jumps, and drunk or sober he has been in more duels than any man I know. It is a wonder he has lived this long.'

'But think of the estate,' said Mama.

It was an entreaty which fooled no one, for she cares very little for the estate and a great deal for her firstborn son.

'If Frederick is fool enough to get in the way of a sword then Henry will look after it,' said my father.

Mama pleaded with him again, but to no avail, Papa's mind was made up.

At last Mama left the room in some distress, closely followed by my father, who was still shouting his dissatisfaction. I, meanwhile, was no less dismayed than Mama. Having no desire to inherit the estate, I was not pleased with the turn events had taken.

'Have a thought for me,' I said to Frederick, as he staggered drunkenly to his feet. 'I do not want to inherit Northanger Abbey, I would much rather inherit the family living. So take care of yourself. I do not want to see you take a bullet.'

He smiled broadly.

'Henry, dear boy, so there you are. It's good to see you,' he said, breathing brandy fumes into my face. He looked at me narrowly as he swayed on his feet, and added, 'all of you.' Poking me affectionately in the chest, he went on, in a slurred voice, 'You're a good man, Henry, a very good man. You're not just my brother, you're my best friend and I love you, I do. So I will tell you something, Henry. Now listen carefully. Come closer. Closer. Never give your heart to a woman. Never, never, never. Promise me. Promise me!'

'I promise.'

'Good. Good. Because they are devilish creatures, all of them. They lead a man on, they say they will love him for ever, and then do you know what they do? Do you, Henry? They leave him for his best friend. And do you know why they do that? Because his best friend has more money. They are not worth a candle. They are heartless and loveless and good for nothing. I will never love any woman ever again. I am glad to be going into the army. No women in the army. It's the army for me, Henry my boy.'

He tried to stand up but lurched drunkenly and saved himself by putting his arm around my shoulder.

'We men must stick together,' he said.

Then his arm began to slide from my shoulder, he slipped down beside me and passed out on the floor.

When he is sober, my brother looks wicked and dangerous, when he is drunk he has the look of a cherub. His face relaxed and a happy smile curves his lips.

I was loath to break up such a pretty picture, but knowing what was likely to come next I rang the bell for his valet. Together we managed to lift Frederick to his feet and then we half-carried, and half-walked, him to his room where we put him to bed.

Friday 16 April

My sister Eleanor who, at the age of thirteen, is promising to become a beauty, was amused when I told her about the morning's events, particularly by the possibility of my becoming the heir.

'On, no, Henry! You cannot inherit the estate!' she said, laughing, as she gambolled through the gardens in front of me, taking joy in the early-spring sunshine. 'You will never make a good heir. You are not nearly reckless or rakish enough.'

'I had the same thought myself. It is essential, I suppose, for heirs to be reckless and rakish?' I asked her.

'You know it is! You have read as many novels as I have – well, almost! It is unthinkable to have a son and heir who is a sober and reliable person. He has to spend his life seducing virtuous young women, or drinking himself into a stupor, or placing bets on whether he can drive from London to Brighton in seventeen minutes and forty-two seconds—'

'Which of course he manages to do, though the distance is at least fifty miles and the feat is impossible.'

'And he has to turn good, honest families out of their homes when he has nothing better to do, and then give their houses to his mistresses ...'

'... even though the good, honest families are so virtuous that they have attended church every Sunday for their whole lives ...' I said.

'... and so poor that they have nowhere else to go, and will therefore die in the snow,' finished Eleanor. 'Now Frederick is a very good first-born son. He is wild and handsome and he comes home drunk every night, and he is always losing money over some ridiculous bet. But you would make a very bad squire, for you have never done any of these things.'

We turned along the chestnut walk.

'Not yet, I grant you,' I said. 'But in the unlikely event of my ever inheriting, I shall try to give satisfaction. I don't suppose that I can become a rake all at once, but I will take it in stages. I will begin by making a mildly scandalous remark to the Lowrys' governess, perhaps commenting on her shapely ankles. I will make a similar small beginning on gambling, betting five shillings on whether or not it will rain on Saturday, and proceed from there.'

Eleanor laughed and ran through into the walled garden, where we were sheltered from the wind.

'You will never make a good villain,' she said. 'You will have to resign yourself to being a hero.'

'I have been thinking just the same thing, for I have the necessary dark eyes and rather dark hair. Alas, honesty compels me to mention that I do not have a hero's height, nor his noble mien nor his wounded heart.'

'You are still growing, I suppose, so you will be taller by and by. Your mien is noble enough, in a dim light. As for your lack of a wounded heart, that is because you have not yet met your heroine,' she told me.

'Heroines are hard to find. I have looked everywhere but I have never yet met one.'

'Miss Grey was looking at you in church the other day.'

'But Miss Grey is a bold young woman with brown hair. And heroines, as you know, have golden hair and blue eyes and they are demure in their manners. Their personalities, too, are of a very particular type. They spend their infant years nursing a dormouse—'

'Or feeding a poor, starving canary—'

'Or watering a rose bush, which repays their kindness by transforming itself from a straggling stick into a bush covered in rampant flowers. Yet I have never met such a one. Young ladies nowadays seem to spend their time playing cricket with their brothers or climbing trees, instead of lisping nursery songs to their prettily wounded animals.'

'What a sorry place the world is! If you have not met such a paragon of virtue by the advanced age of sixteen, then I am forced to admit that you possibly never will,' she said with a sigh.

'I have resigned myself to a lifetime of celibacy for that very reason. Without a heroine who has been a part of my life since our cradles, until she is mysteriously sent away to unknown relatives following the death of her parents, there is no hope of happiness for me.'

'There is, perhaps, one possibility which you have overlooked,' she said, pulling a book out of her pocket. 'I believe that, occasionally, heroines are to be met with on holidays abroad.'

She danced into the arbour, where she sat down on a bench and turned her book over in her hands.

'How foolish of me,' I said, sitting down beside her. 'Now why did I not think of that? I will take a walking holiday in Italy as soon as I am old enough to arrange my own adventure.'

She opened her book.

'What is it this time?' I asked her. 'Milton, Pope, Prior? A paper from the *Spectator*, perhaps, or a chapter from Sterne? Or is it a copy of *Fordyce's Sermons*?'

'No,' she said, laughing. 'It is something much better. It is *A Sicilian Romance*.'

'What? A novel?' I asked, affecting horror.

'A novel,' she assented.

'And is it very horrid?' I asked.

'I certainly hope so.' She thrust it into my hands. 'You may read to me as I sew. I have to finish hemming this handkerchief. Mama says she will deprive me of novels altogether if I do not pay more attention to my needlework.'

And out of her pocket she drew needle, thread, and the handkerchief.

'It is a good thing you are still in your schoolgirl's dresses, for such large pockets will be a thing of the past when you start wearing more fashionable clothes – which will not be too long now, I think. You are very nearly a young lady.'

'Pooh!' she said. 'Now read to me, if you please!'

'Very well. But I see you have already begun.'

'Not really. I have only read the first few pages, where the narrator says that he came across the ruins of the castle Mazzini whilst travelling in Sicily, and that a passing monk happened to lend him an ancient manuscript which related the castle's history.'

'A noble beginning. And who lives in this castle? The heroine, I presume?'

'Yes. Her name is Julia.'

'And does she have any brothers and sisters?'

'A brother, Ferdinand, and a sister, Emilia.'

'I am glad to hear it. Brothers are always useful. Their mother is dead, I suppose, driven to an early grave by their cruel and imperious father? And he has married again, a woman who is jealous of her beautiful stepdaughters, but likes her stepson because he brings his handsome friends home?'

'Have you been peeking?' she asked me suspiciously.

'My dear sister, I do not need to peek to know that. A novel would not be worth reading without those essential facts.'

'Well, you are right. And now the stepmother has persuaded the father to go on holiday with her, taking only Ferdinand and leaving Julia and Emilia at the castle in the care of their poor, dear departed Mama's friend – Madame de Menon.'

'Very well. So now I will begin:

'*A melancholy stillness reigned through the halls, and the silence of the courts, which were shaded by high turrets, was for many hours together undisturbed by the sound of any foot-step. Julia, who discovered an early taste for books, loved to retire in an evening to a small closet in which she had collected her favourite authors. This room formed the western angle of the castle: one of its windows looked upon the sea, beyond which was faintly seen, skirting the horizon, the dark rocky coast of*

Calabria; the other opened towards a part of the castle, and afforded a prospect of the neighbouring woods.'

'I am glad she likes to read,' said Eleanor, 'but I wish something horrible would happen.'

'Your wish is about to be granted,' I said.

'On the evening of a very sultry day, Julia, Emilia and Madame de Menon, having supped in their favourite outdoor spot, the coolness of the hour, and the beauty of the night, tempted this happy party to remain there later than usual. Returning home, they were surprised by the appearance of a light through the broken window-shutters of an apartment, belonging to a division of the castle which had for many years been shut up. They stopped to observe it, when it suddenly disappeared, and was seen no more.

'Madame de Menon, disturbed at this phenomenon, hastened into the castle, with a view of enquiring into the cause of it, when she was met in the north hall by the servant Vincent. She related to him what she had seen, and ordered an immediate search to be made for the keys of those apartments. She apprehended that some person had penetrated that part of the edifice with an intention of plunder; and, disdaining a paltry fear where her duty was concerned, she summoned the servants of the castle, with an intention of accompanying them thither.

'Vincent smiled at her apprehensions, and imputed what she had seen to an illusion, which the solemnity of the hour had impressed upon her fancy.

'Madame, however, persevered in her purpose; and, after a long and repeated search, a massey key, covered with rust, was produced. She then proceeded to the southern side of the edifice,

accompanied by Vincent, and followed by the servants, who were agitated with impatient wonder.

'*The key was applied to an iron gate, which opened into a court that separated this division from the other parts of the castle. They entered this court, which was overgrown with grass and weeds, and ascended some steps that led to a large door, which they vainly endeavoured to open.*

'*All the different keys of the castle were applied to the lock, without effect, and they were at length compelled to quit the place, without having either satisfied their curiosity, or quieted their fears.*

'*After several months passed, without further disturbance or discovery, another occurrence renewed the alarm. Julia had one night remained in her closet later than usual. A favourite book had engaged her attention beyond the hour of customary repose, and every inhabitant of the castle, except herself, had long been lost in sleep. She was roused from her forgetfulness, by the sound of the castle clock—*'

We jumped, as the stable clock struck the hour, and then we laughed. But we had been recalled to the present. Eleanor knew her governess would be waiting for her. Reluctantly I closed the book, promising to read to her again later.

I went to the stables and was soon on horseback, enjoying my freedom. I miss it when I am at school, and like nothing better than roaming over the estate on a spring day.

Frederick was looking sober as we sat down to dine, but otherwise morose and pale. Despite his bravado I think he is not happy about going into the army, and there is some deeper wound. If Miss Orpington has disappointed him – and I can think of no other meaning to his words – then I am sorry for him. It is clear to see that he feels it most keenly, for although on the surface he is a rake, I am convinced that he is at heart a romantic.

Mama ate very little and Papa was concerned, asking her if she felt quite well. She said that it was nothing, just her bilious complaint, and that he must not be concerned.

I believe that he is concerned, though, inasmuch as he has it in him to be concerned for anyone.

Saturday 17 April

It is as I feared. Mama was ill again this morning and did not leave her room. Papa blamed it on Frederick. Frederick bore our father's rants with a curled lip, but as soon as Papa went off to examine the kitchens, Frederick's bravado disappeared and he hastened to Mama's room, where he endeavoured to cheer her, and sounds of laughter could soon be heard.

This afternoon he rode over to the Dawsons, saying he was going to borrow something from Peter. He returned with a red coat, Peter being in the army, and went upstairs to show it to Mama. But she was by then feeling unwell, and he was unable to see her. Papa said he would send for the physician tomorrow if she is no better.

Eleanor spent the afternoon sewing diligently, so that she will have something to show Mama when Mama is feeling well again. Being disposed to help Eleanor in her noble endeavour, I took up *A Sicilian Romance*.

'Oh, yes, Henry, please do read to me,' she said. 'I do not know how it is, but a novel is always more enjoyable when it is shared.'

'By which you mean you are afraid to turn the pages by yourself, lest Julia should discover a skeleton in the southern reaches of the castle.'

'I am frightened of no such thing.'

'Of course not. Very well, then, where did we leave it? Ah, yes, Julia was reading late one night and was moving to her chamber, when the beauty of the night attracted her to the window.

'*She opened it; and observing a fine effect of moonlight upon the dark woods, leaned forwards. In that situation she had not long remained, when she perceived a light faintly flash through a casement in the uninhabited part of the castle. A sudden tremor seized her, and she with difficulty supported herself.*

'*In a few moments it disappeared, and soon after a figure, bearing a lamp, proceeded from an obscure door belonging to the south tower; and stealing along the outside of the castle walls, turned round the southern angle, by which it was afterwards hid from the view. Astonished and terrified at what she had seen, she hurried to the apartment of Madame de Menon, and related the circumstance.*

'*The servants were immediately roused, and the alarm became general. Madame arose and descended into the north hall, where the domestics were already assembled. No one could be found of courage sufficient to enter into the courts; and the orders of Madame were disregarded, when opposed to the effects of superstitious terror. She perceived that the servant Vincent was absent, but as she was ordering him to be called, he entered the hall.*

'*Surprised to find the family thus assembled, he was told the occasion. He immediately ordered a party of the servants to attend him round the castle walls; and with some reluctance, and more fear, they obeyed him. They all returned to the hall, without having witnessed any extraordinary appearance; but though their fears were not confirmed, they were by no means dissipated.*

'The appearance of a light in a part of the castle which had for several years been shut up, and to which time and circumstance had given an air of singular desolation, might reasonably be supposed to excite a strong degree of surprise and terror.

'In the minds of the vulgar, any species of the wonderful is received with avidity; and the servants did not hesitate in believing the southern division of the castle to be inhabited by a supernatural power.

'Too much agitated to sleep, they agreed to watch for the remainder of the night. For this purpose they arranged themselves in the east gallery, where they had a view of the south tower from which the light had issued. The night, however, passed without any further disturbance; and the morning dawn, which they beheld with inexpressible pleasure, dissipated for a while the glooms of apprehension.

'But the return of evening renewed the general fear, and for several successive nights the domestics watched the southern tower. Although nothing remarkable was seen, a report was soon raised, and believed, that the southern side of the castle was haunted. Madame de Menon, whose mind was superior to the effects of superstition, was yet disturbed and perplexed, and she determined, if the light reappeared, to inform the marquis of the circumstance, and request the keys of those apartments.'

'Do you think it is really haunted?' asked Eleanor.

'Who can say? It seems only too likely,' I said. 'I can think of no other reason for a mysterious light. There can surely not be a rational explanation of so strange a thing?'

'And do you think Madame will really ask the marquis for the keys?'

'I think she may very well ask him, but whether he will give them to her is quite another matter.'

'Poor Julia,' said Eleanor, with a pleasurable shiver, 'to live in a haunted castle. I am glad the abbey is not haunted.'

'Are you sure? I believe I saw a mysterious light in the kitchen last night,' I remarked.

'Oh, that was just Mama's maid making her a little something,' said Eleanor.

At talk of Mama she fell silent. Reading her thoughts, and knowing she was worried about Mama, I invited her to go riding with me, but she would not be distracted from her needlework.

Frederick was still wearing his red coat when I went upstairs to dress for dinner. He was just emerging from Mama's room, where he had met with a smiling reception, for Mama was feeling somewhat better. He looked remarkably handsome and he was pleased that Mama had said so.

Papa was less pleased to find that Frederick had been to her room, saying, 'Your mother is too ill to be disturbed.'

'On the contrary, she was feeling much recovered and needed someone to take her out of her thoughts,' Frederick remarked. 'She said that red is a very good colour and suits me.'

'It is a very good colour for disguising blood, anyway,' said Papa, 'and there will be plenty of that when you see some action.'

Frederick scowled and said that, as he had worn the coat into town this afternoon it had already seen some action, a remark which incensed Papa. But Frederick laughed at his anger. I did not like to hear it. There was something bitter about the laughter, something cynical. I hope it will not last. Frederick is not made for bitterness and cynicism. I hope his disappointment has not soured him. I am sure it has not. He is too young to abandon all hope of meeting a heroine of his own.

Sunday 18 April

Mama was well enough to join us at church and, apart from being a little pale, was so well that Papa felt able to go ahead with his plan of driving me over to Woodston this afternoon.

'I am glad to see that you are not following in your brother's footsteps,' said my father as we set out. 'A clergyman needs to be sober and respectable and I think I can rely upon you to be both. You have a propensity to humour and you have a love of the absurd, both of which you should attempt to curb, but I am pleased with you nonetheless, Henry. I will be glad to give you the living of Woodston when you are old enough for it. You will not become ordained for many years, but Woodston will be waiting for you.'

He wanted no reply, and so whilst he talked I was free to observe the countryside, with its hints of the coming spring. The drive was agreeable and the twenty miles went by quickly.

'Woodston is larger than it was the last time I was here,' I said. 'There are more chandler's shops, and some new houses, too.'

'It is becoming more prosperous,' my father agreed. 'Its situation is good and its people are hardworking. You will have sensible parishioners and you will be able to make your mark here. I foresee great things for you, Henry, my boy.'

We reached the further end of the village and my father pulled up in front of the parsonage.

'There it is. What do you think of it, Henry?'

I was surprised at his question. We have been to Woodston many times before, but it was the first time he had sought my opinion.

'A little run down, perhaps, and small, but well enough,' I said.

'You think so? I cannot agree with you. In fact, I am very disappointed in the place. I have been growing more and more dissatisfied with it for some time. It is small and dark, and has a mean look about it. I think I am going to have it pulled down and have a new parsonage built in its place.'

I was astonished, but a moment's reflection showed me that I should not be surprised. There is very little left to do on the abbey and my father must always be altering something. Goodness knows what he will do with himself when everything is done.

'The drive needs altering. What do you say? A semicircular sweep would look well, I think. Do not you?' He did not wait for me to answer but continued: 'Good, good, I knew you would approve. It needs a pair of imposing gates to make the entrance worth looking at. Then, with an impressive sweep and a stone-built parsonage beyond, it will be passable. Inside, it will need spacious rooms, well shaped, with windows reaching to the ground. What do you think? The view of the meadows beyond is pretty enough. Perhaps that tree could be moved.'

He set the carriage moving again and drove on to the church, which we reached in time for the evening service.

'The roof has just been replaced,' he said as we climbed out of the carriage, 'and that window will be refitted. I have always thought it a pity it has no coloured glass. There is room for improvement there. We will replace it with a scene from the New Testament. Or perhaps the Old. What do you think? Yes, yes, you are right, David and Goliath, or perhaps the Battle of Jericho.'

The Reverend Mr Wilkes caught sight of us at that moment and set his servant to take care of the horses as he made us welcome. We were the object of some attention as we took our place in the family pew. I liked the atmosphere of the church, it was calm and peaceful. I looked about me at the venerable stonework and the carved oak, which had been made mellow by the countless generations worshipping there. My father's eyes roved around with quite a different view, seeking out things to be altered, and lingering now and then on an ugly bonnet or a battered cane, which I knew he was tempted to remove and replace.

As we waited for the sermon to begin, I wondered whether my heroine might be found at Woodston, and thinking she might be hiding her light under a poke bonnet I endeavoured to read every face. But I saw no one over the age of seven or under the age of forty.

The service at last began. It was tolerable, but I found myself to be my father's son, for I saw room for improvement, and I wrote my own service in my imagination as I listened. Alas, my sermon contained much that was humorous, and I think my father would have been horrified if he could have read my thoughts. But I see no reason why sermons should not be entertaining as well as instructive, and I feel it will be my duty to make sure that my parishioners remain awake whilst I am speaking, instead of falling asleep.

After the service was over we were invited to stay at the rectory by the Reverend Mr Wilkes. My father, having expected the invitation, had made sure we had travelled prepared. We were soon at the parsonage, and then we were left alone whilst Mr Wilkes went to instruct his housekeeper on preparing our rooms.

'You see now why a clergyman needs a wife,' said my father. 'Mr Wilkes is a bachelor and he has to see to all the arrangements himself. When the time comes I will find you an heiress, someone whose wealth will enhance your own and give you an opportunity to make as many improvements as you desire.'

It did not seem sufficient reason to take a wife to me, but I did not want to anger my father and so I did not say so.

Whilst we waited for Mr Wilkes to return, Papa looked around the parsonage with a critical eye.

'Yes, yes, knock it down and start again, there is nothing else to be done. The rooms are too small, and although that wall could be knocked out, there is nothing I hate so much as a patched-on bow. The windows, too ...' He shook his head in disapproval at the small-paned windows, which let in little light. 'But with the new parsonage, you will have nothing to be ashamed of, it will be a gentleman's residence, I can promise you that. Everything in the newest style, well fitted out, the sort of home you can be proud of.

'You will not be dependent on the living, of course, you have your own fortune, but it is important that you have occupation. It is essential for a young man. You are intelligent enough to know what I am talking about. I am not worried for you, Henry. It is your brother who fills me with unease. He never seems to belong to anyone. You are close to your sister, but Frederick has no such close friendship in the family. He loves his mother, as who would not? But that is not the same as having someone in whom he can confide. Confound it, there is something eating the boy, but the devil of it is, I do not know what it is.'

I ventured that it might be a woman.

'What, not Miss Orpington? I thought I had cured him of that. She was not good enough for the heir of Northanger Abbey, and when I sent him into the library I felt sure he would see it for himself.'

'The library?'

'Yes, the library. She was busy flirting with one of Frederick's less savoury friends in there. I am surprised that Frederick expected anything better from either of them, I never expected him to take it so much to heart, but I could not let him continue in ignorance. He had better get over his ill humour before Saturday. We are having some of our friends and neighbours to supper and I will not tolerate his being rude to them. Miss Plainter will be there, along with her brother Charles, and Miss

Maple. We will have some improvised dancing after supper, nothing formal. I will make sure there are musicians there, and then it can all be done on the spur of the moment.'

The Reverend Mr Wilkes returning at that moment, the talk moved on to parish business until we retired for the night.

As I went upstairs I could not help wondering which friend had played my brother false. I do not know them all, but I know of three who are richer than he is, and none of them as worthy of love as Frederick. Miss Orpington must be intolerably stupid, and I cannot help thinking that he has had a lucky escape.

Monday 9 April

We returned to the abbey this afternoon and Papa set about organizing the musicians for the supper party. Frederick was out riding. Mama was feeling much better and was sitting in the parlour with her needlework. Eleanor was sitting beside her with a piece of sewing in her lap, fidgeting.

'There you are, Henry,' said Mama, giving me her cheek to kiss. 'Did you enjoy yourself at Woodston?'

She listened attentively whilst I told her all about it and then said with a smile, 'You will oblige me greatly if you will take your sister out of doors. She is fidgeting terribly.'

The day was indeed lovely and I could tell that Eleanor longed to be outside.

Eleanor jumped up, but then said nobly, 'I will stay here with you, Mama, if you prefer. I can help you with your needlework.'

'Heaven forfend!' said Mama. 'I want to have it finished by dinner time and if you remain by my side it will never be done! Off you go, child.'

Eleanor needed no more urging and we were soon outside. The weather being fine, we went down to the arbour and I was not surprised when she drew out her book. Feeling lazy, I said, 'I think, today, you should read to me.'

'Very well.'

She had scarcely settled herself on the bench when she took up the book and began to read. Her face glowed and her eyes widened as she discovered the horrors within:

'*It was about this period that the servant Vincent was seized with a disorder which increased so rapidly, as in a short time to assume the most alarming appearance. Despairing of life, he desired that a messenger might be dispatched to inform the marquis of his situation, and to signify his earnest wish to see him before he died.*

'*The progress of his disorder defied every art of medicine, and his visible distress of mind seemed to accelerate his fate. Perceiving his last hour approaching, he requested to have a confessor. The confessor was shut up with him a considerable time, and he had already received extreme unction, when Madame de Menon was summoned to his bedside. The hand of death was now upon him, cold damps hung upon his brows, and he, with difficulty, raised his heavy eyes to Madame as she entered the apartment. He beckoned her towards him, and desiring that no person might be permitted to enter the room, was for a few moments silent. His mind appeared to labour under oppressive remembrances; he made several attempts to speak, but either resolution or strength failed him.*

'*At length, giving Madame a look of unutterable anguish, "Alas, madam," said he, "Heaven grants not the prayer of such a wretch as I am. I must expire long before the marquis can arrive. Since I shall see him no more, I would impart to you a secret which lies heavy at my heart, and which makes my last moments dreadful, as they are without hope."*

'I knew it,' said Eleanor. 'I always suspected Vincent. I am sure it was he who carried the lantern. He must be the source of the mysterious lights.'

'I seem to remember your being convinced the castle was haunted.'

'I never said any such thing,' she said comfortably, before returning to the book.

'"Be comforted," said Madame, who was affected by the energy of his manner, "we are taught to believe that forgiveness is never denied to sincere repentance."

'"You, madam, are ignorant of the enormity of my crime, and of the secret – the horrid secret which labours at my breast. My guilt is beyond remedy in this world, and I fear will be without pardon in the next; I therefore hope little from confession even to a priest. Yet some good it is still in my power to do; let me disclose to you that secret which is so mysteriously connected with the southern apartments of this castle."

'"What of them!" exclaimed Madame, with impatience.

'Vincent returned no answer; exhausted by the effort of speaking, he had fainted. Madame rang for assistance, and by proper applications, his senses were recalled. He was, however, entirely speechless, and in this state he remained till he expired.'

'Oh, no!' I cried, clutching my chest and rolling my eyes, much to Eleanor's amusement. 'What horrible secret does he take to his grave?'

She returned to the book impatiently, but she had no chance to read further, for it was time to dress for dinner, and the wicked marquis himself could not be more fearsome than my father when one of us is late.

Tuesday 20 April

Papa watched Mama at breakfast time and he was pleased to see that she ate well, her bilious attack being over, and that she took pleasure in her letter from her old schoolfriend Mrs Hughes, which she read aloud to us with her customary animation. He told her of his plans for dancing on Saturday and she approved of them. Frederick scowled, knowing it was for his benefit and not being in the mood for dancing. However, he said nothing. For the time being, at least, he does not risk open rebellion because my father has agreed to pay his debts of honour, and so Frederick must behave.

'I think, you know, it is time for Eleanor to start joining us for evening gatherings, at least those that take place at the abbey,' said Mama.

Eleanor sat up, alert.

'She is far too young,' said Papa.

'Not so. She is not a child any more, she is turning into a young lady. I do not say she should join us for the dancing, but I think she should join us for supper. It will do her good to see how adults conduct themselves in company and it will give her a chance to practise her manners.'

'She is forever jumping up, she will never manage to sit still,' said my father.

Eleanor became as still as a statue and folded her hands in her lap in the most ladylike fashion imaginable.

'I think we can trust her to manage for a short while,' said Mama.

Papa grumbled some more but at last he let Mama have her own way. Eleanor and Mama exchanged smiles.

'But you will need something new to wear,' said Mama to Eleanor. 'You cannot appear at supper in any of the dresses you already have. We will go shopping this afternoon and look for muslins. We will need some good washing muslin – you are growing so much that you will soon need some new day dresses, and we might as well buy the fabric when we are there – and also something finer for the evening. I think we have time to make something simple for Saturday.'

It was all arranged. Eleanor sketched and practised the pianoforte in the morning, with not one grumble, and I went out riding with Charles Plainter.

Afterwards, we had a light luncheon and by two o'clock the carriage was at the door.

By that time Mama was looking pale again and Papa said she should not go. Mama was adamant, however, but she did not look very strong and so I offered my services as escort.

'Thank you, Henry, a man's arm is just what I need,' said Mama.

She leant on me heavily as we went out to the carriage and said very little as it pulled away from the abbey. The journey was not too long and we went straight to the linen draper's. Mama took a seat whilst we waited for the two people before us to be served.

There were some pretty fabrics on the counter and I looked them over.

'I think that would suit you very well,' I said to Eleanor, nodding towards a green fabric.

Mama smiled indulgently.

'That is satin, Henry, quite unsuitable for a young girl.'

'Then what of the one next to it?' I asked.

'No, that is silk. We want muslin. See, there is a bale of it at the end of the counter.'

The assistant was by that time ready for us. Mama held a knowledgeable conversation with him. I attempted to learn, but I succeeded only in throwing Mama and Eleanor into gales of mirth when I tried to help them choose.

'This is a muslin, I know it is,' I said, indicating one of the fabrics. 'Pray tell me then, why it will not do.'

'Because it will not wash well,' said Mama. 'It will fray. Now this, on the other hand, will wash very well. Do you see the difference?'

I could see it when she told me what to look for and I earned a look of approval when I spotted another good washing muslin.

'Now, as to the pattern, a sprig is suitable for a young girl.'

'A sprig?'

'Like this one. Do you see the pattern, there are small sprigs of flowers scattered across the fabric.' She told the assistant we would take it. 'Now we need something plain white for evening.'

'This one,' I said, picking up a robust muslin.

'That is not fine enough for evening wear,' she said. She examined the other fabrics the draper had brought out for her to admire. 'This one, I think,' she said at last, holding it against Eleanor. 'We will have four yards. No, we had better have more rather than less, we will have five. We can always turn the left-over pieces to some account or other; it will do for a handkerchief, or a cap, or a cloak. Muslin can never be said to be wasted.'

I thought we were done, but Mama and Eleanor spent another hour in the shop and then went in search of shoe roses and a new fan before we were finished.

We returned home and Mama rang for tea.

'Now, tell me what you have been doing whilst I have been in bed,' Mama said, as tea was brought in.

Eleanor spoke at length, telling Mama all about the handkerchiefs she had sewn, the hours she had spent practising the pianoforte and the numerous sketches she had made.

'And numerous novels read, I suppose?' asked Mama, seeing *A Sicilian Romance* lying on the window seat.

'Only one novel. Henry has been reading to me,' said Eleanor.

'Has he indeed. It is not unsuitable, I hope?' Mama asked, going over to the window seat and retrieving the book.

'Not at all,' I said.

'Well, well, I think I will be the judge of that. You may continue to read.'

She put the book in my hands, and I noticed that the bookmark had moved.

'Have you been reading ahead without me?' I asked.

Eleanor looked at me innocently.

'No, of course not,' she said.

'Then how is it that you are more advanced than when I left?'

'Well, perhaps I have read a few pages,' she admitted.

I held them between my finger and thumb and showed her the thickness of 'a few pages'.

'Well, nothing has happened,' she said, excusing herself, 'except that the marquis has returned and has dismissed Vincent's ramblings as nonsense. And when Madame said that she had seen strange lights in the uninhabited part of the castle, he said it was nothing but the delusions of a weak and timid mind.'

'Did he indeed?' asked Mama. 'Madame sounds like a sensible woman to me, but I do not think I like this marquis.'

'His wife is even worse,' said Eleanor eagerly.

'And what of our heroine, Julia, and her brother?' I asked. 'Particularly her brother. Brothers are very important people, and I must know what he has been doing.'

'He has just returned to the castle, too, to celebrate his majority. You will like to hear what the author says of him,' she said, hanging over me and pointing out the passage. 'Look.

His figure was tall and majestic; he had a very noble and spirited carriage; and his countenance expressed at once sweetness and dignity.'

I assumed the air of Ferdinand, standing up and drawing myself up to my full height, whilst doing my best to adopt a countenance of sweetness and dignity, and Mama laughed.

'Bravo,' she said.

I sat down again, took out the bookmark and began to read:

'In the evening there was a grand ball; the marchioness, who was still distinguished for her beauty, and for the winning elegance of her manners, appeared in the most splendid attire. Her hair was ornamented with a profusion of jewels, but they were so disposed as to give an air rather of voluptuousness than of grace to her figure. Although conscious of her charms, she beheld the beauty of Emilia and Julia with a jealous eye, and was compelled secretly to acknowledge, that the simple elegance with which they were adorned, was more enchanting than all the studied artifice of splendid decoration.'

Eleanor gave a happy sigh, no doubt imagining herself as Julia.

'Well, this is certainly good,' said Mama. 'Simple elegance is always preferable to studied artifice.'

'At twelve the gates of the castle were thrown open, and the company quitted it for the woods, which were splendidly illuminated. The scene appeared enchanting. Nothing met the eye but beauty and romantic splendour; the ear received no sounds but those of mirth and melody. The younger part of the company formed themselves into groups, which at intervals glanced through the woods, and were again unseen. Julia seemed the magic queen of the place.

'The Count Muriani was of the party. He complimented the marchioness on the beauty of her daughters; and after

lamenting with gaiety the captives which their charms would enthral, he mentioned the Count de Vereza.'

'The Count de Vereza – Hippolitus – has been admiring Julia, and the marchioness's heart has been corroded with jealous fury,' Eleanor helpfully explained.

'Dear me,' said Mama.

I continued:

"He is certainly of all others the man most deserving the lady Julia," said Count Muriani. "As they danced, I thought they exhibited a perfect model of the beauty of either sex; and if I mistake not, they are inspired with a mutual admiration."

The marchioness, endeavouring to conceal her uneasiness, said, "Yes, my lord, I allow the count all the merit you adjudge him, but from the little I have seen of his disposition, he is too volatile for a serious attachment."'

'She is making that up,' said Eleanor crossly.

'I thought she might be,' said Mama, with a smile at me.

'At that instant the count entered the pavilion,' I went on.

"Ah," said Muriani, laughingly, "you were the subject of our conversation, and seem to be come in good time to receive the honours allotted you. I was interceding with the marchioness for her interest in your favour, with the Lady Julia; but she absolutely refuses it; and though she allows you merit, alleges, that you are by nature fickle and inconstant. What say you – would not the beauty of Lady Julia bind your unsteady heart?"

"I know not how I have deserved that character of the marchioness," said the count with a smile, "but that heart must

be either fickle or insensible in an uncommon degree, which can boast of freedom in the presence of Lady Julia."'

Eleanor gave a dreamy smile.

'Well, it is all innocent enough,' said Mama approvingly. 'You may read it with my blessing. But now I think I will have a rest before dinner. I am a little fatigued after our exertions.'

'I wonder if there will be any counts at the supper party on Saturday,' said Eleanor.

'About a dozen, I should think,' I said, 'and they will all be ensnared by your charms. Indeed I think it certain that they will all be fighting over you, for the heart must be either fickle or insensible in an uncommon degree, which can boast of freedom in the presence of Eleanor.'

'Now you are laughing at me,' she said, but she was beaming with happiness.

I left her to her daydreams and, making the most of the fine weather by calling my dogs, I went down to the river to do some fishing. The sport was good and I caught three fine specimens which were served up at dinner.

Wednesday 21 April

Eleanor and Mama spent the day sewing, aided by Mama's maid. Frederick was still lying low, and I rode over to the Maples. Stewart was at home and Charles Plainter was there. All three of us rode down to Copse End.

'My sister is looking forward to the supper party,' said Stewart. 'Mama wants her to marry Frederick.'

'She is too late. Frederick is going into the army.'

'Yes, I had heard something about it. Been behaving too wild, has he? I thought as much. But nothing so trifling as that will stop Mama,' he said. 'She and Pen are determined to have him.'

'No amount of determination will make Frederick do something he does not want to do,' I said. 'Frederick goes his own way. He ... ' I was going to say that he had had his heart broken, and then decided against it. '... does as he pleases.'

'Will you be there?' asked Stewart.

Charles said that he would be there with his family, whilst I said that I would be there for supper, but not afterwards.

'I have escaped, too,' Stewart said. 'I have to attend the parties at our own house but Mama says that I am still too young to go to our neighbours for evening parties, for which I thank God. I wish I could stay sixteen for ever. Supper parties are bad enough, but dancing is worse. Give me my horses and dogs, my old clothes, let me do as I please and I am happy, but stuff me up in all that rig and make me play the courtier and I am miserable.'

I was not entirely of his way of thinking.

'I like company, if it is good, but too often it is tedious. Everyone says the same things over and over. However, my sister Eleanor will be having supper with us, it is her first grown-up party, and her delight will carry me through.'

Thursday 22 April

Papa has spent the day harrying the servants, making sure that everything will be ready for Saturday. One of his old friends, the Marquis of Longtown, is coming and my father wants to make sure everything is perfect. Mama and Eleanor have again been sewing, and Frederick at last seems to be coming out of himself. He suggested that we should go riding this afternoon, and although I had already been out this morning I obliged him. He talked to me a great deal, about his fears for the future, his disappointment in love and his feeling of purposelessness.

'What use is an heir before he inherits?' he asked. 'There is nothing for him to do.'

'Except go into the army,' I said. 'Perhaps you will like it.'

'It will at least get me away from here. The general will never hand over the reins whilst he has breath. If I had enough money I would buy a place of my own.'

'Then marry an heiress,' I said lightly. 'Stewart says his sister has set her cap at you.'

'What, Pen Maple?' he asked incredulously, reining in his horse, and then he began to laugh.

I had not heard him laugh since his disappointment and I was very pleased to hear it. His horse danced beneath him, snorting, as if to join in the amusement.

'Yes, both she and her Mama are determined to have you,' I said, stopping beside him.

'Penelope Maple is the last woman on earth I would marry,' he retorted.

'You have still not forgiven her for beating you at sledging down the back hill when you were eleven then?' I asked.

'Did she? I had forgotten that.'

'Surely not. You must remember the terrible trouble she was in when her mother discovered she had taken a tray from the kitchen and used it as a toboggan.'

He roared with laughter.

'So she did,' he said.

'Does that make you look more kindly on her?' I asked.

'Of course. I will marry her tomorrow,' he said.

'You could do worse,' I remarked.

The laughter left his eyes and his mood became dark.

'I could do better,' he said.

He set off again, trotting at a sombre pace. His gaiety had gone and although I tried to bring it back again I did not succeed.

Saturday 24 April

The abbey was full of activity today as the house was prepared to receive our guests. Mama took to her room this afternoon to rest and Eleanor, full of energy, darted from room to room, unable to settle in her excitement at the idea of attending her first grown-up party.

'You will wear a hole in the carpet,' I told her. 'Do sit down.'

'Henry! How can you sit still?' she asked me.

'Easily. Come and sit down, bring *A Sicilian Romance* and we will see what is happening to Julia now that she is in love with Hippolitus. Will she win him, or will her evil father and even more evil stepmother ruin her happiness for ever?'

'I hope that Julia and Hippolitus get married and live happily ever after,' she said.

'It will be a very short story if they do. Ah, here is Julia, thinking of her One True Love:

'She was roused from her state of visionary happiness, by a summons from the marquis to attend him in the library. She found him pacing the room in deep thought, and she had shut the door before he perceived her. The authoritative severity in his countenance alarmed her, and prepared her for a subject of importance.

"I sent for you, my child," said he, "to declare the honour which awaits you. The Duke de Luovo has solicited your hand. An alliance so splendid was beyond my expectation. You will receive the distinction with the gratitude it claims, and prepare for the celebration of the nuptials."

'This speech fell like the dart of death upon the heart of Julia. She sat motionless – stupefied and deprived of the power of utterance.

'The marquis observed her consternation; and mistaking its cause, "I acknowledge," said he, "that there is somewhat abrupt in this affair; but the joy occasioned by a distinction so unmerited on your part, ought to overcome the little feminine weakness you might otherwise indulge. Retire and compose yourself."

'These words roused Julia from her state of horrid stupefaction.

'"O! sir," said she, throwing herself at his feet, "forbear to enforce authority upon a point where to obey you would be worse than death. Hear me, my lord," said Julia, tears swelling in her eyes, "and pity the sufferings of a child, who never till this moment has dared to dispute your commands."

'"Nor shall she now," said the marquis. "What, when wealth, honour, and distinction, are laid at my feet, shall they be refused, because a foolish girl – a very baby, who knows not good from evil, cries, and says she cannot love! Accept the duke, or quit this castle for ever, and wander where you will."

'Saying this, he burst away, and Julia, who had hung weeping upon his knees, fell prostrate upon the floor. The violence of the fall completed the effect of her distress, and she fainted.'

'Of what use was that?' asked my sister unsympathetically.

'Do you not think you might faint, if you were in her predicament?' I asked.

'I never faint,' she declared. 'I think Julia ought to run away with Hippolitus.'

'It seems that Hippolitus is of your mind,' I said, continuing, 'for Hippolitus suggests that very thing. And Ferdinand, that most noble of brothers, agrees that it is the only way to happiness.'

Eleanor seized the book from me in her eagerness and read,

'They now arranged their plan of escape; in the execution of which, no time was to be lost, since the nuptials with the duke were to be solemnized on the day after the morrow. It was settled, that if the keys could be procured, Ferdinand and Hippolitus should meet Julia in the closet; that they should convey her to the seashore, from whence a boat, which was to be kept in waiting, could carry them to the opposite coast of Calabria, where the marriage might be solemnized without danger of interruption.'

I read over her shoulder as she fell silent in her perusal of the lovers' miraculous escape to the shore, but we did not read at the same speed and so I reclaimed the book, continuing to read aloud:

'"Now, my love," said Hippolitus, "you are safe, and I am happy."

'Immediately a loud voice from without exclaimed, "Take, villain, the reward of your perfidy!"

'At the same instant Hippolitus received a sword in his body, and uttering a deep sigh, fell to the ground. Julia shrieked and fainted—'

'Again,' said Eleanor, not impressed with Julia's fortitude.

'Ferdinand, drawing his sword, advanced towards the assassin, upon whose countenance the light of his lamp then shone, and

discovered to him his father! The sword fell from his grasp, and he started back in an agony of horror. He was instantly surrounded, and seized by the servants of the marquis, while the marquis himself denounced vengeance upon his head, and ordered him to be thrown into the dungeon of the castle.

'Julia, on recovering her senses, found herself in a small room, of which she had no remembrance, with her maid weeping over her. Yet her misery was heightened by the intelligence which she now received. She learned that Hippolitus had been borne away lifeless by his people, that Ferdinand was confined in a dungeon by order of the marquis, and that herself was a prisoner in a remote room, from which, on the day after the morrow, she was to be removed to the chapel of the castle, and there sacrificed to the ambition of her father, and the absurd love of the Duke de Luovo.'

I closed the book dramatically and said, 'And now, it is time to dress.'

'Oh, no!' said Eleanor.

'Oh, yes! You cannot be late for your first supper party.'

'But poor Julia! What is to become of her?'

'What indeed?'

'Do you think she will be forced to marry the duke?'

'It seems to be the lot of heroines to be forced into unhappy marriages,' I said.

I stood up and walked towards the door, whilst Eleanor danced along beside me.

'I wonder if I will be sacrificed to the ambition of my father when I am older?' said Eleanor with interest.

'I think it most likely,' I said with a smile.

'Then I must hope I fall in love with a good and wealthy man like Hippolitus before that happens.'

'It is possible, of course, that you will meet someone like Hippolitus,' I said, as we went upstairs. 'I do not quite despair of it. But I fear it is more likely that you will marry a man who appears to be good and wealthy, but turns out to be poor and villainous.'

She nodded.

'I dare say, once we are married, he will reveal that he is in fact a pauper, rob me of my small marriage portion and then lock me in a dungeon. And yet I must marry.'

'Why?'

'I cannot live here all my life,' she said.

'That is true enough. But I will have a living when I go into the church. You can come and live with me.'

'That idea suits you now,' she said, 'but when you have met your heroine, the two of you will not want a third.'

'My wife will love you as I do.'

'No, she will only pretend,' said Eleanor. 'But she will secretly resent me. When you are away she will slowly poison me, or lock me in the attic—'

'Or both.'

'Very likely. And when you return to the parsonage she will say that I have been called away to nurse an old schoolfriend.'

'I will accept her story. But then I will start to hear strange noises. I will ask her about the groaning coming from the attic....'

'... and she will say it is the second housemaid, who has a toothache.'

'And I will believe her. I will only discover that it is you, my dear sister, when it is too late. Thinking at last that there is something very strange about so prolonged a toothache, I will unlock the attic door....'

'... where nothing but my skeleton will remain to greet you.'

'Alas, what a cruel fate awaits you, dear Eleanor. But an even crueller fate will await you this evening if you are late, so hurry up and get ready.'

She disappeared into her room, and I disappeared into mine, both of us emerging in good time to welcome our guests.

Frederick earned Mama's gratitude by pretending not to recognize Eleanor in her grown-up dress, and saying, 'I beg your pardon, Mama, I did not know that our guests had started to arrive. And who is this beauty?'

Eleanor wriggled in delight, and said, 'It's me!'

At which Frederick pretended astonishment and told her she would outshine every other lady at the table.

Papa looked her up and down with a critical eye but then said, 'You will do very well,' which pleased her greatly.

Our guests began to arrive and they all greeted her with a friendly air. Pen Maple told her how pretty she looked and Charles Plainter said she was an adornment to the gathering.

To Eleanor, the meal was the most interesting imaginable; to the rest of us I fear it was dull. Penelope was in good spirits and sought to entertain Frederick, who made an effort to exert himself to begin with but then relapsed into silence, at which Penelope exchanged a glance with her mama and reconciled herself to entertaining an elderly dowager; Papa spoke at great length of his many improvements, which interested our guests for about five minutes and then steadily drove them into a stupor; Mama seemed unwell and although she was a perfect hostess she lacked her usual vitality; Charles drummed his fingers on the table until his mother caught his eye, whilst I endeavoured to entertain our guests, with small success.

I was grateful to leave the company after supper, and as I left the room, Charles said to me in an aside, 'I envy you, Henry, I wish I could escape. Supper parties are the most tedious affairs.'

I am of Charles's and Stewart's opinion: give me my dogs and my horses and I am happy, but make me endure another such supper party and I will be tempted to leave for Calabria.

Sunday 25 April

Mama was tired and spent the day in bed; Eleanor was dull, a reaction to the excitement of last night; Frederick went out as soon as we returned from church without saying where he was going; Papa amused himself by showing his many improvements to his friend, who dealt with this imposition by talking of his own improvements whilst taking no notice of anything my father said. In this way they were both happy. I made the most of my last few days of freedom and went out with my dogs.

Only a few more days and I will have to return to school.

Tuesday 27 April

Mama was much recovered, and saw to the household as usual. She gave instructions for the packing of my boxes and went through all my clothes herself to make sure they would last me the term. I am sorry to be leaving Northanger and my family, but looking forward to seeing my friends again.

When the ladies had withdrawn after dinner, Papa gave me his fatherly advice for the coming term: that is, not to spend more than my allowance, and to behave like a gentleman. Since I have never done the former, and have always done the latter, his advice was unnecessary, but nevertheless it was well meant.

Eleanor presented me with the handkerchief, which she has now finished hemming.

'I did not know this was for me.'

'Neither did I! I did not know if I would finish it in time, but

now that it is done, I give it to you with love and thanks. It will
be very dull here without you.'

'You still have Mama.'

'Yes, I know, and I am thankful for it.'

I took the handkerchief with many thanks and put it in my
trunk. So tomorrow it is back to school for me, and I will not see
the abbey again until the summer.

JULY

Monday 12 July

This is not the homecoming I expected. The abbey is hushed, the
servants walk about with frightened faces and Papa gives them
contradictory instructions every half-hour. Mama was taken ill
yesterday and is in bed. She refuses to let Papa send for Mr Leith,
the physician, but if she is no better by tomorrow, Papa means to
send for him anyway.

Tuesday 13 July

I am glad Mr Leith is here, and I am persuaded that Mama is glad,
too, for she likes him and she trusts him. He spent the morning
with her, but this afternoon he found me in the library and told
me that she was asking for me.

'She is very weak,' he said. 'Her bilious attacks are severe and
almost constant. She is enjoying a brief respite at the moment but
I fear it will not last long. I cannot disguise from you the seriousness of her condition. Say nothing to distress her. Speak quietly

and do not let her tire herself. Your brother is with her at the moment, but you may go up in a few minutes. It is unfortunate that your sister is away from home. She is visiting your aunt, I understand?'

'Yes. I had a letter from her this morning,' I said. 'I will read it to Mama.'

'Good. Well, I think you may go up.'

I went upstairs. As I approached Mama's room, Frederick was just coming out. He was visibly upset. I started to speak but the words died on my lips. He looked at me sorrowfully and then stood back to let me pass.

The curtains were drawn and the room was dark. I went over to the bed and was shocked to see how drawn she looked. But she smiled when she saw me and I did what I could to lift her spirits, entertaining her with a few tales of school and then reading her Eleanor's letter.

'I am so glad I sent her to stay with your Aunt Ann,' said Mama, sinking back on her pillows. 'It is not easy for her here, being the only girl, and when you and Frederick are away it is even more difficult, for she is very much on her own. This stupid illness of mine has made it impossible for me to spend as much time with her as I would wish. So I was very pleased when your Aunt Ann invited her to stay, though Scotland is such a long way away. But it seems the journey was worth the effort, for she is evidently having fun with her cousins. It does me good to hear of her trimming bonnets and looking through fashion plates like other girls of her age.'

She gave a wan smile, but then her face contorted and she waved me away. The sound of her illness followed me out of the room.

Wednesday 14 July

Mr Leith called in two of his colleagues this morning and all three of them remained in almost constant attendance on Mama, doing what they could to alleviate her suffering, which was intense. They became more and more concerned as the day wore on, until at last they told Papa that Eleanor should be sent for, if he wanted her to have a chance of seeing her mother again. Papa sent a letter at once, and then paced the garden without once looking at any of the transformations he had wrought. I went into the chapel and, being unable to help Mama in any other way, I prayed.

Friday 16 July

It is as I feared. Mama's attack of the bilious fever was much worse this time and she suffered a seizure in the early hours of this morning. Though I can scarcely believe it, she is dead. The abbey is in mourning. The servants weep quietly and Papa is seriously affected. Frederick is subdued and I feel lost. But it is even worse for Eleanor. Poor child! To be away from home at such a time. There is now no chance of her seeing our mother again, unless it is to see her in her coffin.

AUGUST

Monday 2 August

Eleanor is home, the funeral is over, and the household is returning to normal, if anything can ever be considered normal again.

I am worried about Eleanor. I picked up our copy of *A Sicilian*

Romance today and found that Eleanor had turned back the corner of one of the pages we had already read:

One day, when Julia was arranging some papers in the small drawers of a cabinet that stood in her apartment, she found a picture which fixed all her attention. It was a miniature of a lady, whose countenance was touched with sorrow, and expressed an air of dignified resignation. The mournful sweetness of her eyes, raised towards Heaven with a look of supplication, and the melancholy languor that shaded her features, so deeply affected Julia, that her eyes were filled with involuntary tears. She sighed and wept, still gazing on the picture, which seemed to engage her by a kind of fascination. She almost fancied that the portrait breathed, and that the eyes were fixed on hers with a look of penetrating softness. Full of the emotions which the miniature had excited, she presented it to Madame, whose mingled sorrow and surprise increased her curiosity. But what were the various sensations which pressed upon her heart, on learning that she had wept over the resemblance of her mother! Deprived of a mother's tenderness before she was sensible of its value, it was now only that she mourned the event which lamentation could not recall.

Slipped inside the pages at that point was a small miniature of our mother.

I did not like to mention the matter to our father, but I was glad when he told me that Mrs Hughes has offered to visit. Mrs Hughes, being Mama's oldest friend, will know what to do.

Tuesday 3 August

Mrs Hughes arrived this afternoon, full of sympathy and maternal solicitude. She radiated comfort and we were all glad of her presence, Eleanor particularly so. The two of them hugged, and Mrs Hughes listened to all my sister's heartfelt grief with tender pity.

When I could speak to her alone, I showed her the novel. She read the passage and said, 'It is not to be wondered at, but she will feel better now that I am here. I do not think she should read any more Gothic novels, however, at least not for the time being. Motherless heroines are all very well when they are a long way away, but at the moment they are too close to real life for comfort. Some company is what your sister needs, to take her out of her sad thoughts. I will stay for as long as I can, but I think that school would be a good thing. It will give her cheerful companions of her own age. The abbey will be very lonely for her otherwise. I will speak to your papa about it.'

She was as good as her word. I never thought Papa would agree to the idea, but Mrs Hughes represented the virtues of the idea to him and at last he gave way.

I went out riding and when I returned I discovered that Mrs Hughes and Eleanor were in Mama's favourite walk. Eleanor never used to like it, but ever since Mama died she has been drawn to it. I thought it an unhealthy place, with its narrow path winding through a thick grove of old Scotch firs and its gloomy aspect, but when I spoke to Mrs Hughes about it later, saying that I thought it was certain to bring on a fit of melancholy, Mrs Hughes said that some period of melancholy was necessary.

'And what about you, Henry?' she asked.

'Me?'

'Yes, you have lost your mother, too.'

I told her that I was happy, but it was not until she had listened to me for an hour that I realized how devastated I had been. She has done us all good, even Papa, who busies himself more than ever, but who I am sure misses Mama, as do we all. I cannot believe it. I keep expecting her to walk in the room with her customary smile and attend to her needlework, but I know I will never see her again.

Thursday 12 August

Papa called Eleanor into his study this morning and told her that Mama's jewellery would, when she was old enough, be hers. It was a melancholy experience for her to touch the much-loved necklaces and bracelets, but it served to turn her thoughts forward as well as back.

'Papa has promised me the pearls for my come-out,' said Eleanor to me this afternoon. 'They were a gift to Mama from her papa when she married. I have always liked them and I am looking forward to wearing them when I am old enough; they will remind me of her.'

'You will look very well in them, I am sure, and Mama would be pleased. Do you like having Mrs Hughes here?'

'Very much. I am only sorry that she will soon have to leave us, though I understand that her own family need her. But she has promised to visit us again, if Papa is willing, and she says that we must write to each other very often.'

I offered her my arm as we walked through the gardens.

'She has told Papa that he should send you to school, otherwise you will be very much on your own here,' I said.

She clutched my arm more tightly.

'I could not bear to leave Northanger,' she said in a worried voice.

'Not at the moment, perhaps, but in time. You will have company at school, and an opportunity to make friends. Mama met Mrs Hughes when they were both at school, remember. I think it would be good for you, by which I mean, I think it would promote your happiness. I will soon be going back to school myself, and Frederick will be returning to his regiment, which means that, otherwise, you will be left here with Papa.'

She shuddered, knowing Papa's temper to be uncertain at the best of times.

'Perhaps it would be a good idea,' she said. 'And then I could invite friends to stay with me in the holidays as well.'

'An excellent idea. I am glad you have decided to like school. I know Mrs Hughes will be suggesting the idea to you within a very few days, and at least you will now be prepared.'

'Life is not what I thought it was going to be,' said Eleanor with a sigh.

'No, my dear,' I said, putting my hand over hers. 'It never is.'

1798

Friday 26 October

Though I sometimes wish my father were not so restless and not forever altering things, I must confess that the new parsonage is a vast improvement on the old one, and that Woodston is now ideally suited to my needs. The house is large and airy with plenty of light: a gentleman's residence with an imposing drive and entranceway. There is also a small room next to the drawing room where I can keep all my mess and clutter, and where I can have my dogs about me. I told him so this morning when I expressed my intention of moving into it next week.

'That will never do,' he said. 'It is not yet fitted up. There is no furniture in the dining parlour and the drawing room has not even been decorated.'

'I am not thinking of entertaining just yet. The small room next to the dining parlour is fitted out and it is enough for my needs. I can eat there and sit there as well as anywhere else, at least until the rest of the house is ready for use.'

'You would do better to stay here until everything is done, it is far more comfortable and an easy journey.'

'I need to be in my own parish. When I am more established there it will be different, but for the moment I want to set my mark on the place,' I said.

'If it were just a matter of furniture, then perhaps I would agree with you, but there are other improvements to be made and they would be easier to carry out if you were here.'

'As to any further improvements to the parsonage, it has just been built. I cannot think there is any more to be done,' I said.

'Oh, the house, but the gardens are not finished, and there is work to be done on the view. The Carsons' cottage can be seen from the drawing room window, it would be much better to knock it down and build it elsewhere. I have already talked to Robinson about it.'

'Then I must ask you to untalk to him. It is time for me to start managing the place myself, and besides, I cannot ask the Carsons to move their cottage for so small a reason as to improve the view.'

'So small a reason, you call it? When the cottage can plainly be seen amongst the apple trees? I think it a very good reason.'

I knew he would go on arguing, for if I waited for him to be ready for me to move I would wait for ever, and so I cut short his protestations by saying, 'I have already appointed a housekeeper.'

'Have you indeed? And did you not think to consult me about it? But then, you have always been headstrong, and I suppose you must move into the parsonage at some time. But not next week, you had better go next month. We have house guests arriving on Monday, do not forget, and they will be here for the better part of a month. Some of them, my oldest friends, are already here. Your brother will no doubt take over the billiard room as usual with his set of friends. The army has done something to improve him but not as much as I hoped. He is still prone to mix with the wrong company, he needs a wife. I have invited a number of eligible young women and you, too, Henry, should be giving some serious thought to the matter of matrimony. Many of your friends are already married. Charles Plainter is not only married but he has three children.'

'Charles is older than I am.'

'True, but you are four-and-twenty, old enough to be finding someone with a good dowry of twenty or thirty thousand pounds. There is a particular young lady I think you will like, a Miss Barton.'

I will be very surprised if I like Miss Barton, my father's and my tastes on young ladies being exactly opposite, but it will not stop my father from bringing her to my notice at every opportunity.

Eleanor was sympathetic. I found her in the arbour, sheltered from the wind, well wrapped up in her coat and cloak, writing in her journal.

'Do not let me interrupt you,' I said. 'I would not want to get in the way. I hope you are writing of me. Let me tell you what you ought to say: *Henry home, booted and greatcoated – complimented me on my gown – said that blue becomes me – admired the curl of my hair – disturbed me with his nonsense when I would much sooner be writing in my journal.*'

She laughed and put her journal aside.

'I did not expect you back so soon. Have you come to say goodbye?'

'Never goodbye, my dear Eleanor, though you are right, I told our father I would be leaving for Woodston next week. In his usual way he overrode me and the result is that I am to stay for the house party and leave next month. He wishes me to marry Miss Barton.'

'She is very beautiful.'

'And very mercenary. She will not settle for a younger son, and comes only in the hope of seeing Frederick. She will profess herself delighted with the abbey, the neighbours, the countryside, in short everything about us, for the first week. Then, after ten or eleven days, when she learns that Frederick has no interest in her, she will discover that the countryside lacks true beauty; by the end of the second week she will find that our neighbours are boors; by the time the party ends she will be concealing her yawns behind her hands and whispering to the rest of our guests that she will not be sorry to leave.'

'I think our father means us all to find our destinies this month. He has told me on a number of occasions that General Courteney's nephew and the Marquis of Longtown's son are both admirable gentlemen, and that either one of them would make me a good husband. I believe he means to marry me off to one or other of them.'

I sat down beside her.

'Have nothing to do with the Marquis of Longtown's son,' I said. 'He will in time be a marquis himself, and they are always imperious and cruel.'

She laughed, and we were both taken back to a moment eight years ago, when we read *A Sicilian Romance*.

'Did you ever finish it?' I asked Eleanor.

'No, I never read any of it after Mama ...' She fell silent for a few moments and then, rousing herself, said, 'Did you?'

'No,' I admitted. 'We have not been very fair to Julia. We have left her imprisoned in a small room and we have left Ferdinand languishing in a dungeon. Do you never want to know what happened to them?'

'Perhaps, one day.' She looked about her, at the newly replanted arbour, and said, 'A lot has changed since then, but in essentials it is still the same. You have still not found your heroine.'

'Alas, no, despite Papa holding regular house parties in an effort to bring more wealth – I beg your pardon, a heroine – into the family. I will not find her in Miss Barton, that is sure. Do you know who the other guests are to be?'

'Yes, I wrote the invitations myself.'

She named them all, and I gave a wry smile.

'And so, the characters are before us,' I said. 'Eleanor Tilney, heroine; General Tilney, the imperious father; Frederick Tilney, the son and heir, a cynical rake; Henry Tilney, the younger son, an ironic creature with – perhaps – the soul of a romantic; an assortment of gentlemen who seek to take the heroine off to their castles, or at least their residences in the remote reaches of the country; friends of Frederick Tilney, idle and extravagant; a collection of military gentlemen, friends of General Tilney; and an absence of the friends of Miss Tilney and Mr Henry Tilney, who are not considered grand enough for the occasion.'

Eleanor laughed. Then she said, 'Frederick remains as fastidious as ever, and yet he continues to mix with the worst kinds of young men. I think that he is lonely, and yet he rejects every young woman offered to him. I cannot make him out. I sometimes wonder whether he will ever find anyone good enough to be loved by him, for I am certain that that is what is the cause of his problems. Do you think he will find anyone?'

'I begin to despair of it. His early disappointment has given him a morose outlook, and as life has not provided him with any proof that love exists, he takes leave to doubt it. Whereas I – I have not given up hope,' I said.

'I am glad of it. You are not so very old, only four-and-twenty, there is time for you yet.'

'And you, my dear Eleanor, are only twenty. Far too young to be marrying General Courteney's nephew and, at any age, far too good to be marrying the Marquis of Longtown's son. They are here already, I understand.'

'Yes. Papa wanted his particular friends to himself for a few days before the rest of the guests arrived, and their families of course came with them. I am hoping you will render me your assistance in my attempts to avoid them, for they have been following me everywhere I go. Only in the library am I safe if I remain indoors. They never so much as look at a book. But I believe we may be free of them here for a while.'

'When I marry – if I marry – my wife must love to read. I shall make it the one condition. Her dowry is unimportant, her family is irrelevant, but she must be a lover of novels, or else no wedding will take place!'

Wednesday 31 October

It is as I suspected, the house party is dull and if not for Eleanor I should depart for Woodston, whatever my father might say. But I cannot abandon her to such poor company. Frederick speaks to no one except his own particular friends and it is a blessing they keep to the billiard room, for when the door opens, a cloud of smoke and brandy fumes escape, sent on their way by ribald stories and even more ribald laughter. Miss Barton, as I suspected, catches him whenever he is not in the billiard room and flatters him from breakfast to supper, though he treats her with contempt. My father is polite enough, but he promotes his friends' relations at every opportunity, and poor Eleanor is hard put to keep away from them. The only interesting point is that one of Fredericks' guests, Mr Morris, avoids the billiard room and indeed seems to avoid Frederick. He does not in the least look like one of Frederick's friends, lacking a swagger, and having something of the look of a startled deer. Eleanor and I have spent much of our time speculating as to his identity. It is fortunate we have this mystery, for there is little else to entertain us here.

NOVEMBER

Friday 9 November

A surprising day, or perhaps it is better to say a tedious day with a surprising evening. My father was holding forth in the drawing room after dinner and Frederick's friends were in the billiard room, so Eleanor and I took refuge in the library. We had just begun to talk about the marquis's son when there was an embarrassed cough and Mr Thomas Morris stepped out from behind one of the bookcases.

It was an awkward moment. He had evidently been in the library when we arrived and he had unwittingly overheard our conversation. He did not laugh and make some dubious remark, as might be expected from one of Frederick's friends. Instead, he blushed and fingered his collar and muttered his apologies, adding that he had not meant to overhear our conversation but that he had been searching for a book.

This so astounded Eleanor and I that we looked at each other in amazement. Then we turned our eyes back towards him, to discover that he was indeed holding a book.

'The antics in the billiard-room are not to your taste?' hazarded my sister.

'No, I am afraid not,' he said apologetically.

'What book have you found?' I asked.

He looked embarrassed and muttered something under his breath.

'Oh, just something I was reading at home. I thought I had packed my copy but I do not seem to have it with me, and I wondered if I might find a copy here. Luckily I have done so – if you do not object to my borrowing it?'

'You are very welcome to it,' said Eleanor. 'What is it?'

He tucked the book behind his back, but not before Eleanor had glimpsed its cover.

'*A Sicilian Romance!*' she exclaimed.

'I have a partiality for Gothic novels,' he admitted shamefacedly.

'But this is capital,' I said. 'My sister and I like nothing better. Which ones have you read?'

'*Castle of Wolfenbach, Clermont, Mysterious Warnings,* and *Necromancer of the Black Forest,*' he said, warming to his theme. '*Clermont* was my favourite, but I must admit that I find them all very exciting.' Then, recollecting himself, he said, 'But I must not intrude any longer.'

'You are not intruding,' I assured him.

'Will you not join us?' asked Eleanor.

He looked delighted, but then decorum got the better of him and he said sedately, 'If you are sure …'

'We are,' said Eleanor. 'We would like nothing better than some new company, would we not, Henry?'

I was quick to echo Eleanor's sentiment, saying that we would be glad to have him join us.

He looked quietly pleased and took a seat.

'Forgive me for saying so, but you do not seem like one of my brother's friends,' said Eleanor.

He was embarrassed.

'I … uh … I am not exactly his friend, I think it would be more accurate to say that … well, to put it frankly … that is to say … I know him because … well, he owes me money.'

'And he has invited you here in lieu of paying you, I suppose,' said Eleanor with a sigh.

He blushed and fiddled with his cravat.

'My rent being unpaid on account of the loan, which he finds himself temporarily unable to repay, he said it was the least he could do. He invited me to stay for a month, at the end of which he assures me he will be able to meet his obligations.'

'Frederick grows worse,' said Eleanor.

She looked at Mr Morris with a sympathetic eye, and with something else besides. It was curiosity and liking and perhaps even admiration, for his face had a certain interest to it and his manner, if hesitant, was engaging.

'I am very sorry that you have been inconvenienced,' I said, determined to make him feel welcome, 'but for my own part I cannot regret it. Frederick's error has brought us a true companion, and for that we must thank him.'

Eleanor smiled at me and mouthed the words, *Well done*. And indeed the poor fellow needed them, for he was uncomfortable – as who, in his position, would not be?

The conversation seeming likely to die, Eleanor said, 'And where have you got to in *A Sicilian Romance*?'

I was pleased to see her animation and thought that, if Morris could enable her to overcome the sad memories that were attached to the book, then so much the better.

He opened it and showed the place.

'Ah, only a few pages behind us,' I said. 'My sister and I are reading the book also. Pray, catch up with us and then we can read on together.'

I wondered whether Eleanor would object, but after opening her mouth slightly she closed it again.

When he had reached the place we ourselves had reached, he began to read aloud:

'The nuptial morn, so justly dreaded by Julia, and so impatiently awaited by the marquis, now arrived. The marquis and

marchioness received the duke in the outer hall, and conducted him to the saloon, where he partook of the refreshments prepared for him, and from thence retired to the chapel.

'The marquis now withdrew to lead Julia to the altar, and Emilia was ordered to attend at the door of the chapel, in which the priest and a numerous company were already assembled. The marchioness, a prey to the turbulence of succeeding passions, exulted in the near completion of her favourite scheme. A disappointment, however, was prepared for her, which would at once crush the triumph of her malice and her pride. The marquis, on entering the prison of Julia, found it empty!

'His astonishment and indignation upon the discovery almost overpowered his reason. Of the servants of the castle, who were immediately summoned, he enquired concerning her escape, with a mixture of fury and sorrow which left them no opportunity to reply. They had, however, no information to give, but that her woman had not appeared during the whole morning. In the prison were found the bridal habiliments which the marchioness herself had sent on the preceding night, together with a letter addressed to Emilia, which contained the following words:

"'Adieu, dear Emilia; never more will you see your wretched sister, who flies from the cruel fate now prepared for her, certain that she can never meet one more dreadful. In happiness or misery – in hope or despair – whatever may be your situation - still remember me with pity and affection. Dear Emilia, adieu! You will always be the sister of my heart – may you never be the partner of my misfortunes!'"

He read well, and we were both engrossed.

'I am very glad that Julia escaped,' I said.

'And so am I,' he agreed. 'I did not want to see her condemned to marry the duke. A woman should marry for love.'

'Do you really think so?' asked Eleanor.

'I can think of no other reason,' he said.

'And a man?' asked Eleanor.

'The same, or what else is the point of it?'

I liked him more and more.

'Do you think the marquis will be content to let her go?' Julia asked.

He glanced down at the book again and shook his head, saying, 'I fear not, for it says: *It was agreed to pursue Julia with united, and indefatigable search; and that whenever she should be found, the nuptials should be solemnized without further delay. With—*'

The sound of the dressing gong stopped him.

'Oh! I cannot bear it!' said Eleanor in pleasurable horror. 'I hope the marquis does not capture her, or I am sure he will do something terrible to her.'

'But not as terrible as whatever the general will do if we are late for dinner,' I said. I turned to Mr Morris. 'I am sorry, but my father is very particular about timekeeping. We will have to continue with this later.'

'By all means,' he said, looking much happier than he had done half an hour before.

We went inside and dressed quickly, but I was delayed by my cravat and so by the time I arrived downstairs my father was pacing the drawing room, his watch in his hand. On the very instant of my entering, he pulled the bell with violence and ordered, 'Dinner to be on table directly!'

As luck would have it, Eleanor was seated between Mr Courteney and Mr Morris. Whilst Courteney talked of nothing but his horses and his dogs, Mr Morris evidently talked of more interesting things, for Eleanor was absorbed and on several occasions I saw her smile.

Frederick had been instructed to take the sweet and innocent

Miss Dacres in to dinner and I was pleased to see that he treated her with courtesy. It was a relief that he was still able to value goodness and propriety. But he took little interest in her and responded to her comments with scant enjoyment.

My father had ensured that I took Miss Barton in to dinner, whereupon she flirted outrageously with every wealthy man at the table. After dinner she flirted with Frederick in the drawing room and he was in a mood to indulge her, but if she thinks she will catch him, she is mistaken. She is just the sort of woman he has no time for. He said as much when we retired for the night.

'If she chooses to make a fool of herself, that is her concern,' he said. 'Women are fools, all of them.'

'Eleanor is not a fool.'

'Eleanor is a sister,' he returned.

'There are other sisters in the world, are there not? Perhaps one amongst them will be worthy of your love.'

He looked at me pityingly and said only, 'You will learn.'

I was not happy with this reply.

'I wish you would not always see things in such a dark light,' I said impatiently.

'Worried for my heart, little brother?' he asked mockingly.

'That, and my own wellbeing. If you marry, Papa will stop pestering me to do so. With an heir in the cradle he will be content to let me take my time, instead of introducing me to every wealthy or well-connected young woman he knows.'

'And why should that trouble you? You are an admirer of the fair sex.'

'But not at all hours of the day, in all situations. There are times when I do not want to be introduced to yet another damsel who can talk of nothing but her embroidery.'

'So that is what Miss Barton was talking to you about!' he said with a wry smile.

I laughed.

'In Miss Barton's case, I wished she *would* talk of her embroidery! I am as fond of nonsense as the next man, and can talk it by the hour if required, but Miss Barton's kind of nonsense fatigues me, particularly when it is only said for the ears of other men.'

'So, you object to her using you to attract other, wealthier men, dear brother? Your lessons in love have just begun.'

There was no arguing with him and so I took myself off to bed.

Saturday 10 November

The weather being fine, Eleanor and I escaped our guests this afternoon and, warmly wrapped, retreated to the arbour. Glad that she had overcome her aversion to *A Sicilian Romance*, I suggested we continue with it but Eleanor looked conscious and went pink and said she rather thought we might wait.

'Wait? For what?' I asked, though I had more than a passing suspicion.

'Not what. Whom,' she said.

I looked at her with interest.

'Am I to take it that you are expecting Mr Morris?' I asked.

'I happened to mention that we were in the custom of sitting in the arbour when the weather was fine, and I believe he saw us through the window and noticed the direction in which we were heading.'

'And I suppose you also told him he would be welcome to join us?'

'Is he not?'

'My dear Eleanor, you know as well as I do that he is. You are free to invite anyone you wish to join us, and I would suffer a much worse man for your sake. Are you fond of him?' I asked curiously.

'I have only just met him. I hardly know him,' she replied.

'That is not an answer. It is possible to be fond of a person one has only just met, and dislike very strongly a person one knows well.'

'That is very true. I do not wish to commit myself on so short an acquaintance, and so I will say only this: that I find him interesting and pleasant to look at.'

'*Only* this? It is a very great deal, especially from you, who are so particular. It is the curse of the Tilneys to be very particular. We all three suffer from it, you and Frederick no less than myself. I have not heard you say so much in favour of a man since – well, ever.'

'Do you not like him then?' she asked. 'I rather thought you did.'

'He is good company, I will grant you, or I suspect he will be, once he has overcome the last of his shyness. Amusing on occasion. A gentleman in his address. But too easily put upon. How he came to lend Frederick money is beyond me. He must, I think, be deficient in sense.'

'No, not that. Just deficient in the ability to refuse a favour.'

'As failings go, that is a bad one. It is not conducive to happiness. Though I must confess I am surprised at Frederick. He usually borrows money from wealthy men. It is unlike him to stoop so low as to borrow from someone impecunious.'

'As to that, there was some confusion. Mr Morris's uncle is a viscount, and somehow Frederick had mistaken Mr Morris for the viscount's son, a very wealthy young man. There is a family resemblance, it seems.'

'And Mr Morris did not disabuse him of his mistake?'

'When he discovered it, yes. But by then it was too late. The money was already lent.'

'And already spent?' I asked.

'Unfortunately so, which is why Frederick invited Mr Morris to Northanger Abbey, to make amends.'

'But whether that will be a good thing or a bad thing remains to be seen. Papa will not countenance a match, you know. He wants you to marry a man of standing, of great wealth and grand position. Someone who will bring renown to the name of Tilney, and, through marriage, add vast estates to our own.'

'Yes, I know he does, but you go too fast. I have only just met Mr Morris, and although I will confess to having had some conversation with him this morning when you were out with your dogs, I know very little of him and he knows very little of me. There has been no talk of marriage, nor will there be for a very long time, if at all.'

'But it could happen. Guard yourself, Eleanor. I would not want to see you hurt.'

We sat for some time but, as Mr Morris did not appear, Eleanor at last suggested we continue. She read ever more eagerly as we followed poor Julia's adventures, and so engrossed were we that we did not notice the arrival of Mr Morris until he cleared his throat.

I looked at him with new eyes. He was handsome enough, with a good bearing and a neat style of dress; nothing ostentatious and yet not shabby; and I wondered how I felt about the idea of his becoming my brother-in-law. His gaze, as it fell on Eleanor, was rapt, and that was a point in his favour, for anyone who marries Eleanor must adore her to have my blessing.

'Mr Morris. This is a surprise,' I remarked.

He tore his gaze away from Eleanor, who had flushed, and made his bow.

'I hope I am not intruding,' he said.

'Not at all. We hoped you would join us, did we not, Eleanor?' I said.

'We did, indeed.'

He looked surprised and bashfully pleased. This endeared him even more to Eleanor, who invited him to sit down.

'I see you have brought your book with you.'

'I rather hoped we might ... that is to say, it was most enjoyable to share the novel ... I do so enjoy reading aloud ... I thought we might do it again.'

'By all means,' said Eleanor.

'I must confess,' he said, 'that is to say, I could not sleep and so I succumbed to temptation and read some further passages.'

'So did we!' said Eleanor. 'That is, we have read on this morning.'

'Ah! Then you know that Julia, helped by her faithful servant, escaped from the marquis and fled to a convent?' he asked.

'Yes, we do. And do you know about Hippolitus?' I asked.

'That he is alive, having only been severely wounded and not killed? Yes, I know,' he said. 'Also, that he sent an emissary to the castle to discover what had happened to Julia, and, finding that she had escaped, he followed her to the convent – only to find that she had fled the convent when the cruel *Abate* had tried to force her to take the veil.'

'And do you know about Ferdinand?' asked Eleanor.

'That he managed to escape from his father and that he rescued his sister from the convent?' he asked.

'Yes,' said Eleanor. 'And now Julia and Ferdinand are fleeing through the countryside, pursued by their evil father, with Hippolitus trying to find them.'

'That is exactly the point I have reached,' he said.

'Then let us continue,' said Eleanor.

As soon as Mr Morris had seated himself beside us she began:

'Hippolitus gave the reins to his horse, and journeyed on unmindful of his way. The evening was far advanced when he discovered that he had taken a wrong direction, and that he

was bewildered in a wild and solitary scene. He had wandered too far from the road to hope to regain it, and he had beside no recollection of the objects left behind him.

'A choice of errors, only, lay before him. The view on his right hand exhibited high and savage mountains, covered with heath and black fir; and the wild desolation of their aspect, together with the dangerous appearance of the path that wound up their sides, and which was the only apparent track they afforded, determined Hippolitus not to attempt their ascent.

'On his left lay a forest, to which the path he was then in led; its appearance was gloomy, but he preferred it to the mountains; and, since he was uncertain of its extent, there was a possibility that he might pass it, and reach a village before the night was set in. At the worst, the forest would afford him a shelter from the winds; and, however he might be bewildered in its labyrinths, he could ascend a tree, and rest in security till the return of light should afford him an opportunity of extricating himself.'

A wind blew up and ruffled the pages. Eleanor drew her cloak more tightly about her and smoothed the pages down before continuing:

'He had not been long in this situation, when a confused sound of voices from a distance roused his attention and he perceived a faint light glimmer through the foliage from afar. The sight revived a hope that he was near some place of human habitation; he therefore unfastened his horse, and led him towards the spot whence the ray issued. The moonlight discovered to him an edifice which appeared to have been formerly a monastery, but which now exhibited a pile of ruins, whose grandeur, heightened by decay, touched the beholder with reverential awe. Seized with

unconquerable apprehension, he was retiring, when the low
voice of a distressed person struck his ear. He advanced softly
and beheld in a small room, which was less decayed than the rest
of the edifice, a group of men, who, from the savageness of their
looks, and from their dress, appeared to be banditti. They
surrounded a man who lay on the ground wounded, and
bathed in blood. The obscurity of the place prevented Hippolitus
from distinguishing the features of the dying man.'

Eleanor continued to read, but she had to hold the book closer
and closer to her face, for dark clouds began to swarm across the
sky. She was stopped in mid sentence by an ominous rumble. The
sky turned swiftly from blue to black and then the rain began to
fall.

As one we sprang up and ran indoors, where we established
ourselves in the library just as the storm broke. It was so dark that
I lit the candles and we sat around the fire as lightning tore the
sky outside. There was a great clap of thunder and Eleanor
jumped.

We all laughed, and she said, 'This is the perfect weather for
our occupation. But I have read enough. Mr Morris, will you not
read to us instead?'

He took the book hesitantly but the story would brook no
delay and he was soon reading in a strong, clear voice.

'Hippolitus by some mischance attracted the attention of the
banditti. He was now returned to a sense of his danger, and
endeavoured to escape to the exterior part of the ruin; but
terror bewildered his senses, and he mistook his way. Instead of
regaining the outside, he perplexed himself with fruitless
wanderings, and at length found himself only more deeply
involved in the secret recesses of the pile.

'The steps of his pursuers gained fast upon him. He groped his way along a winding passage, and at length came to a flight of steps. Notwithstanding the darkness, he reached the bottom in safety and there he perceived an object, which fixed all his attention. This was the figure of a young woman lying on the floor apparently dead.

'Hearing a step advancing towards the room, he concealed himself and presently there came a piercing shriek. The young woman, recovered from her swoon, was now the object of two of the ruffians, who were fighting over their prize.

'Hippolitus, who was unarmed, insensible to every pulse but that of generous pity, burst into the room, but became fixed like a statue when he beheld his Julia struggling in the grasp of the ruffian. On discovering Hippolitus, she made a sudden spring, and liberated herself; when, running to him, she sunk lifeless in his arms.'

It was at this moment that my father opened the library door and entered with his friends. Mr Morris started. I believe we all, for one moment, expected to see a group of *banditti* standing there. But even *banditti* could scarcely have struck us with more dismay, for my father was accompanied by the Marquis of Longtown and General Courteney, with their son and nephew in tow.

'Ah, there you are,' said our father to Eleanor. 'We have been looking for you, have we not, gentlemen? We are all looking forward to hearing you sing for us.'

'We are indeed,' they said.

Eleanor threw me a beseeching look but I could do nothing to rescue her, for my father drew her to her feet and gave her up to the Marquis's son on one side, and the general's nephew on the other. I followed them to the drawing room, where Frederick looked on with a disdainful eye and Miss Barton amused herself by flirting.

Eleanor went over to the piano and I stood by her, ready to turn her music. Poor Morris took a seat in the corner, a picture of dejection.

I believe we would all three of us have preferred to remain by the fire, whilst the thunder rolled and the lightning cracked, reading to each other.

Sunday 11 November

'And what do you think of Miss Barton?' asked my father this morning, when he met me at breakfast.

The two of us being early risers, there was no one else there.

I did not reply.

'Well, out with it,' he said.

'I presume you mean, what do I think of my marrying her?'

'Of course I do. What, do you think I am asking your opinion of her singing?'

'I do not think she would make a very good rector's wife,' I said.

The comment gave him pause.

'Well, perhaps you are right. Miss Halifax, now, she would make an excellent clergyman's wife. Quiet, respectful and already used to good works. You must drive her somewhere this morning. Show her the local beauty spots. The weather is fine, she will enjoy it.'

'Unfortunately I will be going over to Woodston. I want to make sure there has been no storm damage, and I have to take the afternoon service.'

'Capital! We will all drive over there together. You will be able to see her in the rectory. I am sure you will appreciate her docile nature there. She has a fortune, you know, thirty thousand pounds. It will enable you to make more improvements to the gardens and to extend the grounds. I will make the arrangements at once. We will set out by ten and be there for lunch.'

'It is rather too far to go there and back in a day at this time of year.'

'Nonsense! It will be a moonlit night. Ladies like that sort of thing. They deem it romantic. You can propose to her on the way home.'

There was nothing to be gained by arguing. We duly set out, a small party consisting of my father, the widowed Mrs Halifax, Miss Halifax, myself, Miss Barton – whom, I am convinced, my father has not despaired of as a wife for me, despite her flirtatious character – and General Courteney, with Eleanor seated between the General's nephew and the marquis's son. I am proud to say that she conducted herself admirably. Neither a Julia nor an Emilia could have borne their cruel fate with more nobility.

The day was fortunately more entertaining than I had expected. Miss Barton set her cap at General Courteney, who, although twice her age, is very eligible – and, as she murmured in an aside to me, likely to die quickly and leave her a happy widow.

Miss Halifax murmured politely when Papa pointed out all of Woodston's virtues, but relieved me greatly by telling me, when we walked round the gardens, that she was in love with her local curate. That was the source of her interest in good works! Her mother suspected the attachment and had brought her to the abbey in order to marry her to someone eligible as quickly as possible, so as to crush for ever the curate's pretensions.

'But in less than six months I will be of age. I will come into my fortune and Mama will have no more sway over me. I intend to marry Horace the following day.'

'Then it will do no good for me to propose to you in the carriage on the way home?' I said.

'None whatsoever,' she remarked. 'Were you about to propose?'

'No. But my father intended that I should.'

'Parents are a wonderful thing,' she remarked demurely, but with laughter in her eyes.

One of the horses throwing a shoe, we were home later than expected, and spent the remainder of the evening listening to Miss Halifax play the harp.

'Mama is certain that I appear to great advantage sitting behind the instrument,' she said to me in a low voice as I turned her music for her.

I could not help laughing and her mother, taking it for an encouraging sign, smiled benignly.

It is on such occasions that I wish I were a hundred, then no one would be trying to find me a wife!

Monday 12 November

Having been so cruelly interrupted in our reading on Saturday, we were able to return to it this morning as it was a fine day and most of the party was out riding. It was too cold for us to sit outside, however, and so we retired to the library.

'I can scarcely wait,' said Eleanor. 'I was tempted to read ahead, but determined to wait until we could all read on together.'

Mr Morris took up the book. What was our delight to find that Julia was not dead, but had only fainted. Mr Morris laughed, explaining that he had every sympathy for Julia but thought she could perhaps try to faint a little less often, which amused Eleanor, who warmed to him even more. But then to our horror we learned that the dying man Hippolitus had glimpsed in the small room was none other than Ferdinand, who had been beaten by the *banditti* whilst trying to protect his sister. Hippolitus, however, was more fortunate and managed to escape from the banditti with the fair Julia.

'They wandered for some time among the ruins till they were stopped by a door which closed the passage, and the sound of distant voices murmured along the walls. The door was fastened by strong iron bolts, which Hippolitus vainly endeavoured to draw. The voices drew near. After much labour and difficulty the bolts yielded – the door unclosed – and light dawned upon them through the mouth of a cave, into which they now entered, and from there into the forest.

'They had proceeded about half a mile, when they heard a sudden shout of voices echoed from among the hills behind them; and looking back perceived faintly through the dusk a party of men on horseback making towards them. The pursuers were almost come up with them, when they reached the mouth of a cavern, into which Julia ran for concealment. Hippolitus drew his sword; and awaiting his enemies, stood to defend the entrance.

'In a few moments Julia heard the clashing of swords. She shrunk involuntarily at the sound, and pursuing the windings of the cavern, fled into its inmost recesses. She groped along the winding walls for some time, when she perceived the way was obstructed. She now discovered that a door interrupted her progress, and sought for the bolts which might fasten it. These she found; and strengthened by desperation forced them back.

'The door opened, and she beheld in a small room, which received its feeble light from a window above, the pale and emaciated figure of a woman, seated, with half-closed eyes, in a kind of elbow-chair.

I was alarmed at the effect this might have on my sister, but when I glanced at her I saw that she had not yet guessed at the identity of the woman. Mr Morris, oblivious, read on.

'On perceiving Julia, the woman started from her seat, and her countenance expressed a wild surprise. Her features, which were worn by sorrow, still retained the traces of beauty, and in her air was a mild dignity that excited in Julia an involuntary venera-tion. She seemed as if about to speak, when fixing her eyes earnestly and steadily upon Julia, she stood for a moment in eager gaze, and suddenly exclaiming, "My daughter!" fainted away.'

I looked at Eleanor, but the fainting produced no laughter this time. Instead, Eleanor's face was pale. I wondered whether I should call a halt, but there was a look in her eye which made me remain silent.

'The astonishment of Julia,' read Morris, 'would scarcely suffer her to assist the lady who lay senseless on the floor. A multitude of strange imperfect ideas rushed upon her mind, and she was lost in perplexity; but as she examined the features of the stranger, which were now rekindling into life, she thought she discovered the resemblance of Emilia!

'The lady breathing a deep sigh, unclosed her eyes; she raised them to Julia, who hung over her in speechless astonishment, and fixing them upon her with a tender earnest expression – they filled with tears. She pressed Julia to her heart, and a few moments of exquisite, unutterable emotion followed.

'When the lady became more composed, "Thank heaven!" said she, "my prayer is granted. I am permitted to embrace one of my children before I die. Tell me what brought you hither. Has the marquis at last relented, and allowed me once more to *behold you, or has his death dissolved the wretched bondage in which he placed me?"*

'Truth now glimmered upon the mind of Julia, but so faintly, that instead of enlightening, it served only to increase her perplexity.

"'Is the Marquis Mazzini living?" continued the lady. These words were not to be doubted; Julia threw herself at the feet of her mother, and embracing her knees in an energy of joy, answered only in sobs.'

Morris, looking up at that moment, saw Eleanor's face and, springing up in alarm, said, 'My dear Miss Tilney, you are not well! I will fetch your maid.'

'No,' said Eleanor, recovering herself. 'It is nothing, a slight headache, that is all, but I think I had better lie down for an hour.'

'Of course.'

He offered her his arm but, thanking him, she told him she could manage.

When she had left the room, he expressed his concern again, and thinking it necessary to say something, I told him of the circumstances surrounding the death of our mother.

'I am so sorry, I had no idea, I did not like to ask why Mrs Tilney was not here. And so you were reading *A Sicilian Romance* at the time?'

'Yes, we were. For years it has lain untouched, so that I was very glad when you brought it once again to our notice, and even more pleased that my sister wished to finish it. But I fear that today's reading has been too much for her.'

'As well it might be,' he said with a groan. 'She must have been wishing that she, too, could have discovered that her mother was miraculously alive, and that she could be reunited with her.'

'Alas, there is no chance that my father imprisoned our mother in some secret caves beneath the abbey, or that her funeral was a sham. She has gone beyond recall.'

'I am only sorry that I have been the cause of Miss Tilney's sorrow,' he said.

'You were not to know. Besides, I think it is perhaps a healing sorrow. I hope so.'

'And so do I. You know, of course, that I am in love with your sister?' he asked.

'Yes, I had guessed as much, and I am sorry for you. I am sorry for you both.'

'As for me, I can never be sorry to have met your sister. Do you think there is any chance that your father would listen to my suit?'

'None in the world,' I said. 'I have no wish to pain you, but so it is. Not unless you have any way of making your fortune.'

'Alas, no. I earn a competence, and your sister would be comfortable if she married me – as long as I resist the urge to lend money, which, believe me, is a lesson well learned! – but she would have none of the elegancies of life to which she is accustomed.'

'There is no chance of your inheriting the title from your uncle?' I asked.

'None at all. My uncle has three sons, all in the prime of life and burgeoning with good health.'

'So, short of a freak which would carry all four of your relatives off at once, you have no money, no title – and, I take it, no chance of obtaining any of them?'

'No, none at all,' he said sadly.

'Then if it is at all possible, I beg you to put Eleanor from your mind. There is no hope for you, you know. My father will never consent.'

'I would put her from my mind if I could, but I fear it is impossible.'

I am sorry for it. I like him. But my father will never countenance such a match.

Tuesday 13 November

A letter from Mrs Hughes. It could not have been better timed, for it was handed to Eleanor after breakfast, which she had eaten quietly and with little evidence of pleasure. But she brightened as she opened the letter, and better yet, it contained a suggestion that Eleanor should accompany her to Bath in the spring.

'Capital!' said my father. 'We will all go. It will give you an opportunity to see how happy your friend Charles is with his wife and children,' said my father to me. 'If he could find a wife there, I do not despair of you finding one there, too. My friends Longtown and Courteney mean to take the waters in February and so we will make a party of it. Frederick should be home on leave then as well. We will take rooms in Milsom Street. You will have the shops to entertain you, Eleanor, and you will want to buy some new clothes I am sure. You must look your best at the assemblies. General Courteney's nephew is coming round to his uncle's way of thinking and I make no doubt that he will be willing to make you an offer by Easter.'

This was hardly the kind of thing to make my sister look forward to the visit, and so when my father had departed I said to her, 'Morris is in love with you, you know.'

'Yes, I do know. I had a walk around the garden before breakfast, I wanted some air and I happened to meet him by the arbour. He told me that he would wait for ever if necessary, as long as he knew there was hope.'

'And did you give him hope?' I asked.

'Yes, I did.'

'Is it too late to advise caution?'

'I am afraid so,' she said.

'Well, I do not despair. He will be with us for another two weeks and it is possible that you will discover something to his discredit in that time and change your opinion of him. Let us hope so, at least.'

'I fear there will not be anything,' she said. 'I own I think he is the most charming young man in the world. He was so kind this morning, so generous, so thoughtful. He spoke with such sympathy and such real tenderness that my liking, which has been growing ever since I met him, was elevated to some higher feeling, so that now I know it would be impossible for me to ever marry any other man.'

'It might be impossible for you ever to marry this one.'

'Perhaps. But in a few years' time, when my father sees that I am on the verge of becoming a confirmed spinster, then perhaps he will relent.'

'He is still determined to have you marry one or other of his friends' relations.'

'And I am even more determined not to have them. He cannot force me, or lock me in a cellar, and if by some mischance he finds a series of labyrinthine caverns beneath the abbey and threatens to imprison me there, why, then, I will simply emulate Julia and—'

'Faint?'

She laughed.

'No,' she said, 'escape to a convent.'

'Alas, there are no convents in the immediate vicinity, but you are welcome to escape to Woodston, for I am sure that a parsonage will suit your purposes just as well.'

'And a great deal more comfortably,' she said. 'Very well, if I have need of it, I will take refuge there.'

Wednesday 14 November

Coming upon my sister and Mr Morris in the library, I decided to retreat unseen, leaving them to finish *A Sicilian Romance* together. I retrieved the book after dinner, seeing that they had finished it, and have just now finished it myself. Ferdinand, like Hippolitus before him, had not been killed, but simply injured, and had found his way to his family again. Hippolitus and Julia, of course, were married, and Julia's mother was freed. Thus good was rewarded.

Evil, too, was rewarded when Julia's wicked stepmother poisoned the evil marquis because he upbraided her for being unfaithful, then she rid the world of her own wicked presence by killing herself.

The mysterious light in the castle was caused by the lantern of the servant, Vincent, who had taken food to Julia's mother during her captivity. And it was the marquis, of course, who had imprisoned her and claimed that she was dead, so that he could marry his second wife.

Vincent's pangs of remorse for his evildoing had preyed upon his mind and led to his cryptic comments as he lay on his deathbed, so all was explained. A fine ending to a fine novel!

In real life, alas, things are not so simple. Wives cannot be got out of the way by imprisoning them, husbands cannot be poisoned and good and virtuous heroines do not always marry the men they love. But even so, I hope that my sister's goodness and virtue will in time, by some miracle, be rewarded, and she will be free to marry her Mr Morris.

Thursday 29 November

The house party is nearly over. Our guests will be leaving tomorrow, and I will be removing to Woodston on Saturday.

I wish I could find a young lady I could love half as much as Eleanor loves Mr Morris, but I console myself with the fact that at least I will not have to spend the rest of my life with Miss Barton and Miss Halifax. Though my father has extolled their virtues for the past four weeks, he has not prevailed upon me to make an offer for either one of them.

1799

JANUARY

Tuesday 1 January

With the old year behind me it is my New Year's Resolution to finish the decorating of the parsonage. Eleanor has promised to help me choose the decorations for the drawing room, which is still unpapered, and she has agreed to accompany me to London next week. I am hoping to have the room decorated before we leave for Bath. I have promised to buy her some new novels as a thank you for her help. Since rediscovering the pleasure of Mrs Radcliffe, she now reads all that lady's books avidly, and we are both looking forward to *The Mysteries of Udolpho, a romance, founded on facts; comprising the adventures and misfortunes of Emily St. Aubert,* which promises to be even more horrid than *A Sicilian Romance.*

'And, of course, with such a title, it must be true!' said Eleanor.

'Indeed, for there is no denying that marvellous and terrible things happen all the time. Luckily Mrs Radcliffe seems to know all the details and sets them down for us so that we can enjoy them at our leisure!'

In the meantime I am winning the respect of my parishioners, who were at first bemused by my sermons but, I flatter myself, now find them refreshing. Certainly attendance has gone up since I was ordained and took over the living, and it cannot all be because I am young and unmarried.

Monday 21 January

A most successful trip to London. Some of the papers and paints have been chosen and a pile of novels have been purchased. Eleanor is looking forward to more shopping in Bath.

FEBRUARY

Monday 4 February

My father has arranged to meet his friends in Bath and I have promised to go there next week and take a set of rooms for us. Meanwhile, I must make arrangements for the services when I am absent, for although I will no doubt be returning to Woodston from time to time, I expect to be in Bath for some weeks.

Tuesday 5 February

I wrote to Charles Plainter, telling him that I will be coming to Bath. Since he now lives there it will be a good chance to see him again.

Friday 8 February

A reply from Charles this morning, insisting I stay with him and Margaret until I have found a set of rooms. I sent a note of thanks in reply and I am looking forward to it. The country at this time of year is dreary and Bath will do us all good.

Thursday 14 February

An easy journey and a joyful arrival. Charles's three children ran around me and Margaret welcomed me warmly, saying, 'I am glad you are come, Henry. We have not seen you for an age.'

The house is well set up and Margaret gave me her advice on where to look for my furniture for the parsonage. So did every other lady at the table, and whilst there are few delights in life to match that of speaking of furniture, I was glad when the ladies withdrew and I was left to talk to Charles and his friends.

He asked after Frederick and I told him what I knew, that my brother was on the Continent and I did not know when he would return.

He told me of his family, and we discussed politics and business until we could linger no longer, then we went through into the drawing room to join the ladies.

There was a great deal of nonsense talked, as is customary in Bath. There was a little acknowledgement of enjoyment, but a great deal more ennui, and I could not help thinking that some of those present would be less bored were they not so boring themselves. But I did my duty and entertained those who were capable of being entertained and listened to those who were not.

Much was made of the fact that it was St Valentine's day. Miss Crane and Miss Smith sang songs of maidens languishing for love and knights performing noble deeds, but I suffered their languishing looks in silence, for I was not tempted to slay a dragon, nor even a spider, for either of them.

Friday 15 February

This morning I took a set of rooms for us in Milsom Street and this afternoon went out riding with Charles. This evening we went to the Lower Rooms, which were, for the most part, exceedingly dull. They were full of the usual crowd of people with nothing to say and not a thought between them, but what had been said or thought before. I was introduced to a selection of young ladies by the master of ceremonies, and I obliged them by dancing with them, though there was not one I wished to dance with again, except perhaps Miss Morland. She was new to Bath, having travelled up from the country in company with a Mr and Mrs Allen, and proved to be an entertaining companion. She was not jaded by her surroundings, nor did she pretend to be, and it was entertaining to see how much she enjoyed the bustle, the rooms, the people and the dancing.

Instead of affecting boredom, like the other young ladies, saying that there was not one interesting person to be met with in the whole of Bath, she was charmed, and through her eyes I found that some of the charm of Bath was restored for me. I was amused and pleased with her; so much so, that I invited her to take tea with me. I expected at any moment to be disappointed, as I am usually disappointed, but she did not disgust me by being arch or precocious. She was, if anything, a little too shy, a little too in awe of her surroundings and her company, and I made it my business to tease her into comfort.

After chatting for some time on such matters as naturally arose from the objects around us, I said that I had neglected to ask her how long she had been in Bath; whether she had ever visited before; whether she had been at the Upper Rooms, the theatre, and the concert; and how she liked the place altogether. She said that she liked it very well.

'Now I must give one smirk, and then we may be rational again,' I said.

She turned away her head, not knowing whether she might venture to laugh, but a pleasing smile played about her lips. She was not used to being teased – teasing being in short supply in the country, it seems – and I could not resist the urge to tease her further.

'I see what you think of me,' I remarked. 'I shall make but a poor figure in your journal tomorrow.'

'My journal!' she exclaimed.

'Yes, I know exactly what you will say: Friday, went to the Lower Rooms; wore my sprigged muslin robe with blue trimmings – plain black shoes – appeared to much advantage; but was strangely harassed by a queer, half-witted man, who would make me dance with him, and distressed me by his nonsense.'

'Indeed I shall say no such thing,' she returned.

'Shall I tell you what you ought to say?'

'If you please.'

'I danced with a very agreeable young man, introduced by Mr King; had a great deal of conversation with him – seems a most extraordinary genius – hope I may know more of him. That, madam, is what I wish you to say.'

'But, perhaps, I keep no journal,' she returned, smiling in reply.

'Perhaps you are not sitting in this room, and I am not sitting by you. Not keep a journal! How are your various dresses to be remembered, and the particular state of your complexion, and curl of your hair to be described in all their diversities, without having constant recourse to a journal? It is this delightful habit of journaling which largely contributes to form the easy style of writing for which ladies are so generally celebrated. Everybody allows that the talent of writing agreeable letters is peculiarly female.'

Still she did not dare to laugh, though I was sure she wanted to.

'I have sometimes thought,' she said, 'whether ladies do write so much better letters than gentlemen! That is, I should not think the superiority was always on our side.'

'As far as I have had opportunity of judging, it appears to me that the usual style of letter-writing among women is faultless, except in three particulars.'

'And what are they?' she asked.

'A general deficiency of subject, a total inattention to stops, and a very frequent ignorance of grammar.'

I could tease her no more, for we were joined by Mrs Allen, the woman with whom Miss Morland was staying. Indeed, it was Mrs Allen, along with her estimable husband, who had brought Miss Morland to Bath. Journaling and letter-writing were forgotten and muslins became the subject, on account of Mrs Allen's fearing she had torn hers. She was astonished that I understood muslins.

I told her I understood them particularly well, for I always bought my own cravats, and my sister had often trusted me in the choice of a gown.

'I bought one for her the other day, and it was pronounced to be a prodigious bargain by every lady who saw it. I gave but five shillings a yard for it, and a true Indian muslin,' I remarked.

Mrs Allen was quite struck.

'Men commonly take so little notice of those things,' said she. 'I can never get Mr Allen to know one of my gowns from another. You must be a great comfort to your sister, sir.'

'I hope I am, madam,' I replied.

'And pray, sir, what do you think of Miss Morland's gown?' she asked me.

I looked at Miss Morland and thought it looked uncommonly charming. I could not say so, however, for fear of producing expectations of an early call, or indeed, an offer of marriage. And so I said, 'It is very pretty, madam, but I do not think it will wash well; I am afraid it will fray.'

Miss Morland was laughing now, having decided she could, or having realized that she could not help herself, one or the other. 'How can you,' she said, 'be so—'

I had the delightful feeling she was going to say *strange*, and indeed I was willing her to do so. It would have been amusing to hear such honesty. But she never finished her thought, and Mrs Allen continued to talk of muslins.

I listened politely, though my eyes kept straying to Miss Morland, delighting in her delight at the novelty of her evening. I have been to Bath so many times I had quite forgotten how delightful it can seem to someone who has never been before. So well did I like Miss Morland that when the dancing recommenced I asked for her hand once more.

'What are you thinking of so earnestly?' I asked her as we walked back to the ballroom. 'Not of your partner, I hope, for, by that shake of the head, your meditations are not satisfactory.'

She coloured, and said, 'I was not thinking of anything.'

'That is artful and deep, to be sure; but I had rather be told at once that you will not tell me.'

'Well then, I will not.'

'Thank you; for now we shall soon be acquainted, as I am authorized to tease you on this subject whenever we meet, and nothing in the world advances intimacy so much.'

She looked delighted at the thought, and was too innocent to disguise it, and my evening was more agreeably spent than I had ever expected.

'You look very pleased with yourself,' said Charles, coming up to me.

'Indeed. I have been thinking that it is company that makes the occasion. The Rooms are often tedious but tonight I found them quite charming.'

'It is good of you to say so.'

'My dear Charles, I was not talking of you.'

'Of course not. Who would be charmed by me when Margaret was by?'

'I was not thinking of Margaret, either,' I said. 'You seemed to dance with her half the evening. It is not done, you know. A man should never pay too much attention to his wife.'

'I beg you, leave me one of my pleasures. I can no longer scandalize the neighbourhood by stealing apples and so I must make what scandal I can from the means at my disposal.'

'Very well,' I conceded. 'I give you leave to dance with Margaret as much as you like.'

'You are prodigiously good to me, Henry.'

'My dear Charles, what are friends for?'

Margaret then joining us, we went out to the carriage.

'Who was that young lady you were dancing with?' asked Margaret. 'I thought her rather pretty.'

'I danced with any number of pretty ladies,' I said, as we climbed into the carriage.

'She is new to Bath. I have not seen her before.'

'Ah, *that* young lady. Her name is Miss Morland. She is newly arrived from the country.'

'You made a handsome couple. When you return to Bath with your family, I hope you will dance with her again,' Margaret said.

'When are you returning?' asked Charles.

'Charles! Henry has not even left us yet!'

'No, but I must do so tomorrow, and I hope to return next week,' I said.

'Will Mrs Hughes be coming with you?' asked Margaret.

'Yes, she comes to keep Eleanor company.'

'Good. I will look forward to seeing them both. It seems an age since we met. Eleanor will be astonished to see how much the children have grown.'

The conversation then naturally reverted to the three Plainter sprigs and their remarkable ability to increase their height and girth without any effort at all.

Saturday 16 February

An early start, a good journey and arrived at the abbey in time for luncheon. I told my father and sister about the rooms I had taken. My father was pleased with my description of them and said we will occupy them on Thursday. Then it was back to Woodston for me, where I exercised the dogs, thanked Miss Olsen for the pen-wiper she kindly brought round to the parsonage and then put the finishing touches to tomorrow's sermon.

Sunday 17 February

A good turnout at church today. It had nothing to do with the mild weather and a desire to gossip and everything to do with my oratory skills, I am perfectly convinced. Indeed, if not for Mrs Attwood's new bonnet, I would have had the ladies' undivided attention. The gentlemen I was more certain of. They had no interest in bonnets, new or otherwise, and listened in pleasing silence, broken only by an occasional snore.

Thursday 21 February

Having made arrangements for my absence with Langton, my pleasingly eager curate, I drove over to the abbey where I found Eleanor with her nose in a novel.

'There is no time to read,' I said. 'We must be off to Bath.'

'My father has had to delay our journey on account of business,' she said. 'We do not now go until Saturday, and so I thought I would start one of the books you bought for me in London.'

'I hope it is a good one, for we will need something to entertain us until we leave for Bath.'

'It is excellent,' she said. 'Even better than *A Sicilan Romance*. I believe it is Mrs Radcliffe's best novel.'

I saw the cover and said, 'Ah, you have chosen *The Mysteries of Udolpho*. Excellent.'

She had only just begun, and after allowing me to catch up we read on together, becoming quickly engrossed – so much so, that we could scarcely bring ourselves to put the book down in order to eat. Poor Julia's trials were as nothing to Emily's tribulations. Sinister castles, murderers and *banditti* all conspired to instil terror in our heroine as she travelled through Europe, and we passed the day very pleasantly.

The evening was less pleasant. My father was at home, testy because his business had compelled him to delay our visit to Bath and expressing his dissatisfaction with his doctors and their advice that he should take the waters.

'Stuff and nonsense,' he said. 'But at least some of my friends will be there.'

He did not appear to think it unfair that he had refused Eleanor the pleasure of a friend for company, for although she will have Mrs Hughes, and greatly enjoy her company, she needs companions of her own age, too. But perhaps Miss Morland ... Though some years younger than Eleanor, I think the two of them will like each other.

Friday 22 February

Being eager to continue with *Udolpho*, Eleanor and I set out for the arbour straight after breakfast so as to escape our father's notice. It was no hardship to be out of doors, the morning being sunny, and our being so well wrapped up in coats and cloaks. We were soon thrilling to the adventures of Emily and cursing the evil Montoni. We had just reached the moment where Emily, lifting the black veil, caught a glimpse of what was on the other side and fainted, when my father came into the garden.

'Eleanor! I have here a note, addressed to you, from a Mr Morris. In it, he talks of the house party we held in the autumn. It is, I suppose, the purpose of the rambling note to thank you as hostess of the party, though he expresses himself badly and thinks it necessary to refer to your kindness, your beauty, your humour and your graciousness in every other sentence.' He tapped the note against his other hand and frowned, deep in thought. 'Morris. Morris. I do not remember him. One of Frederick's friends, I suppose. Did you like him?'

'Yes, Father, I did,' said Eleanor, with an expression of hope.

'He was wealthy?' asked my father.

Hope vanished.

'I think not.'

'He has a title perhaps?' pursued my father.

'He is the nephew of a viscount,' I put in.

'Is he?' asked my father with interest. 'And the viscount has no sons?'

'He has three,' said Eleanor, disdaining deceit.

'Oh, in that case ... you must write to him – I will dictate the letter – thanking him for his note but making it clear that any further communication is neither necessary nor desirable.'

Eleanor had no choice but to comply with our father's wishes.

I waited for her as best I could but poor Emily's fate would give me no peace, so after a minute or two I took the novel into the Hermitage walk and devoured it, my hair standing on end the whole time.

Poor Eleanor, when she found me, could not attract my attention, so deeply was I engrossed. When at last I looked up, I could see that she was grieved over the unlucky circumstance of my father intercepting the note but resigned to his reaction, for she had expected nothing better.

'There are times when our father is a regular Montoni,' I said with sympathy.

'I cannot blame my father. I should not have been corresponding with Mr Morris, it is not seemly,' said Eleanor with a sigh.

'Far be it from me to encourage filial disobedience, but the stable boys at Woodston are at your disposal should you need any more notes to be passed.'

'Henry, you are too good to me,' she said with a bright smile.

'I must make amends somehow,' I said.

'For what?'

'For the fact that I have finished the book.'

She looked at me in astonishment.

'Already?' she asked,

'I could not put it down.'

'Well, I forgive you. Tell me, what lay behind the black veil?'

Not wanting to spoil it, I said, 'I think you had better read it yourself.'

She took the novel and was soon lost to the world, everything else forgotten in her perusal of the fantastical adventures of Emily.

Saturday 23 February

There were no unexpected delays and this morning we set out for Bath, arriving at our set of rooms just before noon. My father and Eleanor approved them and we had soon settled in. Mrs Hughes arrived shortly afterwards, having had a good journey, and we exchanged news over tea. Then Eleanor and Mrs Hughes fell to discussing the latest fashions as my father set out to take the waters and I went out riding. The weather was cold and it later came on to rain, but I was glad of the exercise, and after dinner I was able to join with my sister and Mrs Hughes in discussing the merits of long sleeves as compared to short sleeves, for such are now the fashion in Bath.

When the ladies withdrew, my father said that he had commanded Frederick to join us in Bath.

'I cannot see that he has made any great mark in the army,' said my father. 'He is a captain but what is a captain? I expected better from him by now.'

I thought that it would be an uncomfortable meeting when my brother returned.

Sunday 24 February

Church was well attended this morning, despite the rain, and it made a change for me to be in the congregation. The sermon was on the evils of vanity, which did not prevent my sister and Mrs Hughes from making over some of their gowns this afternoon so that they would better suit the prevailing fashions, nor Eleanor from trimming a bonnet.

Monday 25 February

What was my delight this evening to find, when we went to the Upper Rooms, that Mrs Hughes was acquainted with Mrs Thorpe; that Mrs Thorpe was acquainted with Mrs Allen, and Mrs Allen in company with Miss Morland. I was amused to see the last-named smile at seeing me again, instead of pretending not to see me or favouring me with a cool nod, both of which greetings are very much in vogue with the usual young ladies in Bath.

Mrs Allen opened the proceedings by saying that she was happy to see me again, and when we had established that I had only left Bath in order to return with my family she was well pleased, saying that it was just the place for young people.

'I tell Mr Allen, when he talks of being sick of it, that I am sure he should not complain, for it is so very agreeable a place, that it is much better to be here than at home at this dull time of year. I tell him he is quite in luck to be sent here for his health,' she said.

I duly offered my hopes for Mr Allen's health and, good relations being thus established, room was made for Mrs Hughes and my sister to sit down.

Mrs Thorpe's attention was soon turned to her son and daughter, John and Isabella. The latter was dancing with Miss Morland's brother, James. I liked the look of Mr Morland. There was something of the openness of his sister in his expression, for he could not disguise his admiration of Miss Thorpe. It was not to be wondered at, for Isabella Thorpe was exceedingly pretty.

Remembering how much I had enjoyed dancing with Miss Morland before, I offered her my hand, but instead of accepting with alacrity she looked mortified. My pride was salvaged when she explained that she was engaged to Mr John Thorpe for the first dance and so she must decline. Mr Thorpe, however, was nowhere to be seen, leaving his fair partner to sit alone and embarrassed at the side of the room when she should have been enjoying herself. So much for the honour of Mr Thorpe! However, it gave me a pleasing insight into the character of the lady, for it is rare thing in Bath – or anywhere else for that matter – to find a young lady who will forgo a pleasure merely because she has given her word elsewhere. Miss Morland, I felt, was worth knowing.

Thorpe at last arrived. Without a word of apology he said only, 'There you are Miss Morland, I have kept you waiting!' which even a young lady possessed of far less wit than Miss Morland must have already deduced.

I flattered myself that she would rather have had me as a partner, for her eyes kept drifting to me. I remarked as much to Eleanor, who quickly lanced my pomposity and said I was becoming conceited.

'It is not remarkable that Miss Morland should prefer you to Mr Thorpe,' she said. 'Indeed, it would be remarkable if it were otherwise, for I can think of nothing worse than standing up with him. He cannot remember the steps of the dance and does not even try. He has bumped into three different people in the last three minutes, without a word of apology. I will say this for you, Henry, you know how to dance.'

'High praise indeed!'

Eleanor's hand was sought and although the floor was crowded, Miss Morland let her in. I had the satisfaction of seeing them dancing and talking together. I rather hoped Miss Morland would be free for the next dance but she was standing up again with Thorpe, and having been disappointed in my first choice I led Miss Smith on to the floor. Miss Smith, alas, was no substitute for Miss Morland, for if she was not laughing at a young lady who had torn her gown, she was regaling me with an account of her conquests.

'Do you see that gentleman over there, the one with the blue coat? He has told me on three separate occasions how lovely I am and he has five thousand a year. Mama is certain he will offer for me any day. But I do not think I will accept him. I do not like his cravat.'

'Then on no account consider it,' I said. 'It is possible to compromise in certain areas when choosing a partner for life, but never on a cravat.'

She looked at me in admiration.

'That is exactly what I think,' she said. 'You are amazingly clever.'

'It is very good of you to say so.'

'Papa says I am the cleverest girl he has ever met. Captain Dunston remarked upon it as well. But I think he is a very stupid fellow.'

'He must be,' I said; a remark which she did not understand, but which made her smile, for she liked to think of my sharing her opinion of the captain.

At last tea was over, and I found Eleanor and Mrs Hughes in order to take them home. Mrs Hughes exclaimed upon the chance of having met with her friend Mrs Thorpe again. She spoke of Isabella's prettiness and John's fine figure, which last was something of a slander on the word fine, for I never saw such an ill-looking fellow. From there she began talking of her own children, and we were glad to speak of them, for we were both conscious of the great kindness she is doing us by coming to Bath and acting as Eleanor's chaperone.

Back in Milsom Street, Mrs Hughes declared herself tired and retired for the night but Eleanor and I sat up for some time, talking.

'You seemed to be well entertained by Miss Smith,' said Eleanor, as we sat by the fire in the drawing room. 'I saw you laughing twice and smiling often.'

I recounted our conversations and she said, 'Oh dear!'

'And you?' I asked. 'Did you make any new friends? Miss Thorpe, perhaps, or Miss Morland?'

'Miss Thorpe is not to my taste, but I would like to know Miss Morland better,' said Eleanor. 'She has engaging manners.'

'Did you have much chance to speak to her?'

'No, very little, only to exchange commonplaces. We asked each other how well we liked Bath, and talked of how much we admired its buildings and surrounding country. I asked her whether she drew, or played, or sang, and whether she was fond of riding on horseback, and she asked the same of me.'

'And what did you discover?' I asked.

'That she drew, played and sang as much as any other young lady who is not especially accomplished: that is, a little; and that she rides very little as she prefers to walk and there is not always a horse to be got.'

'Well, that is honest enough! Would you like to see more of her, do you think?'

She considered the matter.

'Yes, I think I would. Would you?'

'I?' I asked in surprise.

'Yes, Henry, you.'

'Now what makes you ask that?'

'Because you have spoken of little else since we returned,' she said.

'Am I so transparent? It would seem so. Very well then, I will confess I like her, what little I know of her. She is interesting,' I replied.

'And, moreover, she likes you.'

I was flattered, and thought it was something to be added to Miss Morland's store of virtues. But I did not allow Eleanor to see it.

'She hardly knows me, and what little she does know of me she must think very odd,' I said. 'I talked nonsense to her when we first met, for what else can one talk in the Upper Rooms with someone one has never met before?'

'But oddness is always forgiven in a man who is young and handsome.'

'Be careful or such praise will go to my head.'

'Why? I said that it is forgiven in a man who is young and handsome, I made no mention of you!' she said with a laugh.

It was good to hear it. She has not laughed once these past two months. I am glad we came to Bath.

Tuesday 26 February

My father being busy, Eleanor, Mrs Hughes and I took the air. We had no sooner turned into the Crescent than we met Mrs Allen and Mrs Thorpe. Miss Morland was not with them, but we soon learnt that she had gone for a drive with a small party comprising her brother, Miss Thorpe and Mr Thorpe.

'They are gone to Claverton Down,' said Mrs Allen. 'I am very glad. Catherine needs friends of her own age. I am sure they will all enjoy themselves immensely.'

'And I am sure they will, too,' said Mrs Thorpe. 'I know I am a mother, and partial but I am sure that Catherine could not wish for a better person to drive her than John. He is my idea of what a man should be. He is up at Oxford, you know. I was worried about him at first, for one hears stories of all sorts of things, but he laughs them to scorn. "What? Drinking!" he said to me. "There is no drinking at Oxford now. You would hardly meet with a man who goes beyond his four pints at the utmost. It was reckoned a remarkable thing, at the last party in my rooms, that we cleared about five pints a head. It was looked upon as something out of the common way. Mine is famous good stuff, to be sure. You would not often meet with anything like it in Oxford – and that may account for it. But this will just give you a notion of the general rate of drinking there.'"

'Is not four pints rather a lot?' asked Eleanor.

'Why, I dare say it sounds it to you and me, but John assures me it is not,' said the happy mother. 'He is doing very well for himself. He often buys horses for a trifle and sells them for sums that would astonish you, and he is an excellent shot. Why, the last shooting party he went to, he killed more than all his companions together. Hunting, too, though he has to deal with the mistakes of others in a way you would not credit, and correct the mistakes of even the most experienced huntsmen. And I cannot count the times he has astonished his friends with the boldness of his riding, though I criticize him for this, for although it never endangers his own life for a moment, it leads others into difficulties, and has been the cause of other young men breaking their necks.'

'Dear me,' said Eleanor.

'He sounds a marvel,' I added.

'Aye, I believe he is,' said Mrs Thorpe complacently. 'And my Isabella is no less so. There are always men following her, though she does not give them the least encouragement, and chastises them roundly for it. Why, I have heard her say that she detests young men and the way they give themselves airs, and that she would not encourage them for the world.'

'You are very happy in your children,' said Mrs Allen.

'Yes, I am. But you are happy, too, in your young friends,' she added as an afterthought. 'Catherine is a taking young thing, and her brother James is a gentleman. How did you come to bring them to Bath?'

'We did not bring James, he came of his own accord, but we

brought Catherine. The Morlands are a good sort of family, you know, neighbours of ours, and as we have no children of our own, and as Catherine is of an age to enjoy the balls and parties, and as Mr Allen had to come here on account of his health, we thought she might like it.'

'Well, I dare say she is enjoying herself this morning. My John will see to that. He is the best driver in the world, and he will make sure she has an agreeable outing to Claverton Down.'

Eleanor and I exchanged glances, for we had both seen John drive and thought him likely to overturn his carriage before the week was out. I feared for Miss Morland, and only hoped that the inevitable accident did not occur whilst she was in the carriage.

'We are going to the theatre this evening. Will you be there?' asked Mrs Thorpe.

Mrs Allen said that she and her husband would be there, and Miss Morland with them. Eleanor explained that we had another engagement and we parted company with many professions of good will on both sides.

'Though I would rather be going to the theatre,' said Eleanor this evening, as we went downstairs.

The evening proved to be a trial. My father had invited some of his friends to dinner, and with them came their relatives: General Courteney's nephew, still looking for a wife, and General Parsons's daughter, intent on catching a husband. My father's smiles showed his feelings on the matter and Eleanor and I were left to exercise our wits in evading capture. Eleanor had the worst of it, Mr Courteney feeling at liberty to follow her about, so that she could not avoid him even when she moved from one side of the room to the other. Miss Parsons soon lost interest in flirting with me and turned her attentions to every one of the other gentlemen instead.

Wednesday 27 February

Eleanor and Mrs Hughes went to the pump room this morning, whilst I rode out with my father. He was in a tolerably good mood and said he thought the waters were doing him some good, though I think his improvement has more to do with his pleasure in seeing his friends than in any beneficial effects a few days of drinking the waters might have had.

Returning to Milsom Street we were soon joined by my sister and Mrs Hughes. Whilst my father and Mrs Hughes talked of their mutual acquaintance, Eleanor said to me, 'I saw your Miss Morland in the pump room.'

'*My* Miss Morland?'

'My dear Henry, you must be careful with her. You have awakened her admiration and she is just up from the country, you know.'

'My dear Eleanor, she is safe with me.'

'Yes, I believe she is, which is just as well, for she has a decided preference for you. She had hardly seen me when she said, "How well your brother dances!" She went on to explain, more than once, that she had to turn you down when you asked her to dance, for she really had been engaged to Mr Thorpe the whole day, even though he had not immediately taken her on to the floor. She would not stop talking about you. She had noticed you dancing with Miss Smith, had discovered her name, and asked me if I thought Miss Smith pretty. On my replying, "Not very," she was relieved, and then asked me if you ever came to the pump room. She will be at the cotillion ball tomorrow, and looks forward to seeing you there.'

'Does she indeed?'

'Is it too early for you to have found your heroine?'

'Far too early. I have not yet ascertained whether or not she reads novels and that, you know, is to be the deciding factor in my choice of a bride.'

'I should have thought to ask her,' said Eleanor, 'but never mind, I am sure we will be seeing more of her. She and the Allens are here for some weeks.'

'Is she by any chance like us, without a mother?'

'No. From what I can gather her parents are very much alive, as are her numerous brothers and sisters, but the Allens being childless neighbours and being bound for Bath, they invited Catherine to accompany them. They seem like good people. I like them better than the Thorpes. Miss Thorpe's lips praise Mr Morland, but her eyes invite everyone else.'

'I am sorry for it, he seems likeable enough but we must credit him with the ability to handle his own affairs and we must attend to our own. Do not forget, dear sister, you promised to go shopping with me and help me to find some suitable furniture for the parsonage. The drawing room is still unfurnished, you know,' I said.

After lunch we set out. We had hardly set foot out of the door, however, when we were accosted by John Thorpe, who tried to sell me a horse. When he could not succeed he entertained us with tales of his prowess at every sport invented until he mercifully saw another acquaintance. Thinking this hapless individual might like to purchase his animal, he abandoned us for them.

Eleanor and I were therefore free to investigate the local shops, and although we have not chosen anything as yet, we have seen a dining table and chairs that we both like. I may buy the set if nothing better presents itself.

Thursday 28 February

The morning was spent shopping with my sister and the afternoon riding with Charles and a party of our friends. This evening to the Rooms, where my eyes fell at once upon Miss Morland who was sitting by Mrs Allen with her eyes firmly fixed on her fan. I went over to her and asked her to dance, and was flattered and amused to see with what sparkling eyes she accepted. The dance had scarcely begun, however, when her attention was claimed by John Thorpe, who stood behind her and said that she had promised to dance with him. She protested that he had never asked her but he continued to plague her, saying that he had been telling all his acquaintance that he was going to dance with the prettiest girl in the room. Miss Morland protested that they would never think of her after such a description as that, and what is more, she said it not to invite compliments, as another woman would have done, but because she sincerely believed it. How many young ladies are there who would ever think the same?

Thorpe, with his customary charm, said, 'By heavens, if they do not, I will kick them out of the room for blockheads,' and we were both relieved when the dance swept him away.

I saw that she had been wearied by him, and determined to make her smile again by talking agreeable nonsense to her.

'He has no business to withdraw the attention of my partner from me,' I said. 'We have entered into a contract of mutual agreeableness for the space of an evening, and all our agreeableness belongs solely to each other for that time. Nobody can fasten themselves on the notice of one, without injuring the rights of the other. I consider a country-dance as an emblem of marriage. Fidelity and complaisance are the principal duties of both; and those men who do not choose to dance or marry themselves, have no business with the partners or wives of their neighbours.'

'But they are such very different things!' she said, not knowing whether or not I was serious.

'Then you think they cannot be compared together?'

'To be sure not. People that marry can never part, but must go and keep house together. People that dance only stand opposite each other in a long room for half an hour.'

'And such is your definition of matrimony and dancing? Taken in that light certainly, their resemblance is not striking; but I think I could place them in such a view. You will allow, that in both, man has the advantage of choice, woman only the power of refusal; that in both, it is an engagement between man and woman, formed for the advantage of each; and that when once entered into, they belong exclusively to each other till the moment of its dissolution; that it is their duty, each to endeavour to give the other no cause for wishing that he or she had bestowed themselves elsewhere, and their best interest to keep their own imaginations from wandering towards the perfections of their neighbours, or fancying that they should have been better off with anyone else. You will allow all this?'

'Yes, to be sure, as you state it, all this sounds very well; but still they are so very different. I cannot look upon them at all in the same light, nor think the same duties belong to them.'

I conceded there was a difference, saying, 'You totally disallow any similarity in the obligations; and may I not thence infer that your notions of the duties of the dancing state are not so strict as your partner might wish? Have I not reason to fear that if the gentleman who spoke to you just now were to return, or if any other gentleman were to address you, there would be nothing to restrain you from conversing with him as long as you chose?'

'Mr Thorpe is such a very particular friend of my brother's, that if he talks to me, I must talk to him again; but there are hardly three young men in the room besides him that I have any acquaintance with,' she assured me.

'And is that to be my only security? Alas, alas!'

'Nay, I am sure you cannot have a better; for if I do not know anybody, it is impossible for me to talk to them,' she said with admirable logic; adding, 'Besides, I do not want to talk to anybody.'

I found myself to be surprisingly pleased by her assertion and asked whether she found Bath as agreeable as when I had the honour of making the inquiry before. Upon her replying that she found it ever more agreeable, I reminded her to be tired of it at the proper time, saying, 'You ought to be tired at the end of six weeks.'

'I do not think I should be tired, if I were to stay here six months.'

'Bath, compared with London, has little variety, and so everybody finds out every year.'

'Well, other people must judge for themselves, and those who go to London may think nothing of Bath. But I, who live in a small retired village in the country, can never find greater sameness in such a place as this than in my own home; for here are a variety of amusements, a variety of things to be seen and done all day long, which I can know nothing of there,' she replied.

'You are not fond of the country,' I said.

'Yes, I am. I have always lived there, and always been very happy. But certainly there is much more sameness in a country life than in a Bath life. One day in the country is exactly like another. Here I see a variety of people in every street, and there I can only go and call on Mrs Allen.'

I was very much amused.

'Only go and call on Mrs Allen! What a picture of intellectual poverty! However, when you sink into this abyss again, you will have more to say. You will be able to talk of Bath, and of all that you did here.'

'Oh! Yes. I shall never be in want of something to talk of again to Mrs Allen, or anybody else. I really believe I shall always be talking of Bath, when I am at home again. James's coming (my eldest brother) is quite delightful, especially as it turns out that the very family we are just got so intimate with, the Thorpes, are his intimate friends already. Oh! Who can ever be tired of Bath?'

'Not those who bring such fresh feelings of every sort to it as you do,' I said, and it was true.

Soon after reaching the bottom of the set I saw my father watching me. He asked me about my partner, and seeing that Miss Morland had witnessed the exchange, I told her that the gentleman was my father. She appeared pleased with him, not surprisingly, for he was in a good humour, and talking cheerfully to his friends.

The dance over, we were joined by Eleanor. We fell into conversation about the fine walks to be had around Bath. Miss Morland was eager to experience them but feared she would find no one to go with her, for Mrs Allen was no great walker and Isabella Thorpe would much rather go out in a carriage.

'Then you must come with us,' said Eleanor.

'I shall like it beyond anything in the world!' said Miss Morland with becoming eagerness. 'Do not let us put it off, let us go tomorrow.'

This was readily agreed to. 'As long as it does not rain,' said Eleanor.

'I am sure it will not,' said Miss Morland.

We arranged to call for Miss Morland at her lodgings in Pulteney Street at twelve o'clock and took leave of one another.

'And so, you are to see more of your Miss Morland,' said Eleanor.

'Yes, indeed,' I replied, as we followed my father and Mrs Hughes out to the carriage. 'As long as three villains in horsemen's greatcoats do not force her into a travelling-chaise and four on her way home, and drive her off with incredible speed.'

'In which case you will simply have to rescue her and return her to her lodgings in time to keep her appointment with her friends.'

There was time for no more. My father was already seated in the carriage and waiting impatiently for us to join him.

MARCH

———✦✦✦———

Friday 1 March

Contrary to Miss Morland's belief, it rained this morning and we reluctantly put off our visit to Pulteney Street, but by half past twelve the weather was clearing and after giving it ten more minutes to make up its mind we set out.

As we walked along, with one eye on the sky and another on the puddles, Eleanor said, 'I am very glad to have met Miss Morland and I think that I do her good, too. She has no one to talk to but Isabella Thorpe. From what she has said, Isabella is more interested in young men than in any true friendship, though I think Miss Morland is not yet aware of this. She is used to country manners, where people mean what they say, rather than town manners, where people rarely say what they mean.'

We had just turned into Laura Place when a carriage raced past, driving through a puddle at the side of the road and sending the water flying everywhere.

As Eleanor looked after the retreating carriage in dismay she let out a cry and said, 'Why, it is Miss Morland!'

And indeed it was, being driven at breakneck speed by John Thorpe. He was lashing his horses and sending up spray from the wheels of his carriage like a fountain, soaking the passers by.

'It seems you overestimate Miss Morland's admiration of me,' I remarked.

I took out my handkerchief and made a doomed attempt to wipe the water from my coat as I watched them fly down the road.

'Perhaps it was not her,' said Eleanor, taking my arm as I abandoned my efforts and returned my soggy handkerchief reluctantly to my pocket. 'I only caught a fleeting glimpse, and in such a bonnet, you know, it is hard to tell. We are almost at Pulteney Street, we should call to be sure.'

We walked on, but on our calling at the house, the footman told us that Miss Morland had set out not five minutes since, and that she would not be back all day.

'Has any message been left for me?' asked my sister. 'Miss Tilney?'

'No, miss.'

'Then I will leave my card.'

Finding that she had none about her, we had no choice but to go without leaving one.

'Perhaps we have been wrong about her,' said Eleanor as we returned to Milsom Street to change our wet clothes. 'Perhaps her nature is already changing. Bath has a habit of altering people. A few days ago she would not have broken an appointment, I am sure, but now...?'

'If it is so,' I said, 'then it is better we know now than later. After such a short acquaintance, we will very soon cease to regret her.'

Saturday 2 March

I was eager to escape the city this morning and rode out to the hills, where I worked off the worst of my ill humour in brisk exercise. Eleanor took a walk with my father but when she returned she had some interesting news to give me.

'I was just about to go out with our father when Miss Morland called,' she said. 'The timing was most unfortunate. Papa refused to delay our walk and he insisted on my saying that I was not at home. I do hope she was not offended.'

'We seem to be unlucky where Miss Morland is concerned,' I remarked.

But at the theatre this evening our luck changed, for whom should I espy but Miss Morland. The play concluded, the curtain fell, and on leaving the box I was hailed by Mrs Allen and her friend. I spoke with mere politeness, being out of humour, but not so did Miss Morland reply. As soon as she had a chance she said, 'Oh! Mr Tilney, I have been quite wild to speak to you, and make my apologies. You must have thought me so rude, but indeed it was not my own fault, was it, Mrs Allen?'

It seemed that the Thorpes, eager for her company on an outing, had told her that Eleanor and I would not call so long after the appointed hour, with John Thorpe adding the information that he had seen us leaving town. With such an assurance, and only with such an assurance, Miss Morland had joined her friends on their outing.

I softened towards her, saying teasingly, 'We were much obliged to you at any rate for wishing us a pleasant walk after our passing you in Argyle Street: you were so kind as to look back on purpose.'

'But indeed I did not wish you a pleasant walk,' she said seriously. 'I never thought of such a thing; but I begged Mr Thorpe so earnestly to stop; I called out to him as soon as ever I saw you; now, Mrs Allen, did not – oh! You were not there; but indeed I did; and, if Mr Thorpe would only have stopped, I would have jumped out and run after you.'

Who could resist such a declaration? Not I. I told her it was nothing, that my sister had been disappointed but had trusted there was some reason for it. Alas, Miss Morland would not believe it.

'Oh! Do not say Miss Tilney was not angry, because I know she was,' cried she. 'She would not see me this morning when I called; I saw her walk out of the house the next minute after my leaving it; I was hurt, but I was not affronted. Perhaps you did not know I had been there?'

I admitted that I had known, but explained that Eleanor had been on the point of leaving the house with our father and that he had refused to delay.

She was relieved and then puzzled, saying 'Why, then, Mr Tilney, were you less generous than your sister? If she felt such confidence in my good intentions, and could suppose it to be only a mistake, why should you be so ready to take offence?'

I denied it, but I felt the force of her comment: Bath had not changed her but it had almost changed me. I had been too ready to think ill of her and I was sorry for it. With the misunderstandings cleared away all was well and I joined her in the box and we talked about the play. A comfortable silence falling, her eyes wandered around the theatre.

'How came Mr Thorpe to know your father?' she asked.

I was as surprised as she, but said that my father, like every military man, had a very large acquaintance and I supposed they must have acquaintance in common.

I hoped he had not been inviting Thorpe to dinner. The man is forever bragging about his driving or his billiards or some such thing, and if he is not bragging he is trying to sell me a horse.

We resumed our conversation but the evening was almost over and Miss Morland was spirited away by Mrs Allen. Before we parted, however, we agreed our walk should take place at a later date.

Sunday 3 March

Church this morning – Eleanor good enough to say the sermon was not as interesting as mine – then the King's pump room, where we went to take the waters. They seem to be doing my father some good for he has been in high spirits all day and, for once, concerned about Eleanor.

'I am very glad we came to Bath,' he said. 'I worry about you, Eleanor. You have no company in the abbey, no young women of your own age or thereabouts. You must want someone to talk to.'

I wondered if he had guessed at Eleanor's feelings for Morris and if he was trying to make amends for having dashed her hopes.

'I am not on my own all the time,' said Eleanor. 'Henry visits us as often as he can.'

'Yes, Henry. That is all very well, Henry does his best, but it is not the same as having another female about the place. Did not Miss Morland call the other day?'

'Yes, she did.'

'It was unfortunate that she called just as we were about to leave the house and it seemed better at the time to say that you were not at home, but it was never my intention to come between you and your friend. Look, here she comes now so you may make amends. Henry, a word if you please. Miss Morland, your servant.'

And so saying he drew me to one side so that Eleanor could talk to Miss Morland.

The conversation was of short duration, Miss Morland being with a party of friends, but Eleanor had enough time to rearrange our abandoned walk for tomorrow.

'Splendid!' said my father. 'There is nothing like fresh air for promoting good health and well-being.'

We set out for Milsom Street but we had not been walking for two minutes when Mr Thorpe ran up, looking more like a groom than anything else. He wasted no time on greetings, but said that Miss Morland had sent him to say that she could not, after all, go for a walk on the morrow, because she was engaged to go on an outing with the Thorpes.

'She has only just remembered it, the sad creature!' he said. 'She is going to Clifton tomorrow with us! My sister was quite wild, saying how could Catherine forget her, and so she had better go out with you on Tuesday instead.'

Eleanor was as surprised as I was, but she said, 'Very well, Tuesday is just as convenient for me.'

'I told her it would be! She had better hold tight when I take her out or there will be no knowing what the horses might do!'

And with this, off he went.

As we continued on our way back to our lodgings I could not help wondering whether Miss Morland had sent any such message or if Thorpe had interfered again. The matter was soon settled when, having just reached the house and gone up to the drawing room, the sound of running feet could be heard mounting the stairs. The door opened and there was Miss Morland, having not even waited for William to open the door but having opened the door herself.

She began at once, still breathless from running, and said that it was all a mistake. As I suspected, Thorpe had invented the whole thing. The Thorpes had wanted her to accompany them to Clifton and had not accepted her declaration that she was already engaged. In an act of unwanted officiousness, Thorpe had attempted to rearrange her appointment with us but Miss Morland, brave soul, was having none of it. Regardless of convention she had run after us to set the matter straight. The affair thus happily settled, Eleanor introduced her to my father, who, to my surprise and pleasure, greeted her warmly and apologized to her for having to announce herself.

'What did William mean by it?' he asked. 'To leave you to open the door yourself. I cannot think what he was about. You must think us a sad family, Miss Morland, when we offer you such poor hospitality.'

'No, indeed, it was not William's fault, I came in so quickly and ran by him so suddenly that he could do nothing except follow me up the stairs,' she explained

'Well, if you say so, then we will have to forgive him,' said my father, at his most charming.

Eleanor invited her to sit by her side and asked after Mrs Allen, and my father added his hopes that Mr and Mrs Allen were well.

'They were pointed out to me as most agreeable people,' said my father, 'respectable in every way. We will be happy to make their acquaintance.'

Miss Morland admired my sister's paintings, which were hanging on the wall, and was such a mixture of innocence, vitality and earnestness that I was disappointed when it was time for her to leave.

My father was equally sorry to see her go and invited her to stay and dine with us. She could not accept the invitation, having a prior engagement, but expressed herself willing to come on a future date. Arrangements were made for the day after tomorrow.

My father further surprised me by attending her to the street-door himself, saying 'How well you walk, Miss Morland. Your grace of movement is exactly what I thought it would be when I saw you dancing. We are obliged to you for coming to see us, and we hope to see you again.'

'Is it really the waters?' Eleanor asked me, wondering as much as I did at my father's unexpected good humour. 'I did not expect them to have such a miraculous effect.'

'I can see no other reason for it, unless he has had some good news.'

'But what news could produce such a reaction.'

'Perhaps Frederick is paying court to an heiress?' I said.

'It is always possible,' she returned doubtfully.

'But whatever the reason, I am glad of it, and I only hope it will continue. He has been more used to scaring your friends away than welcoming them in the past. Perhaps he has learnt from his mistakes and now sees that if you are to have company, he must put himself out to be agreeable.'

Monday 4 March

The morning was fair and Eleanor and I called for Miss Morland at the appointed time. We decided to go to Beechen Cliff, just out of town, and were soon walking alongside the river.

'I never look at it,' said Miss Morland, 'without thinking of the south of France.'

I was surprised that she had been abroad, and said so. France these days is no place to visit, or at least, not for anyone who wants to return with their head on their shoulders.

'Oh! No, I only mean what I have read about,' she said.

I could not help smiling when she went on, 'It always puts me in mind of the country that Emily and her father travelled through, in *The Mysteries of Udolpho*.'

Eleanor and I looked at each other, delighted to have found another fellow admirer of *Udolpho*.

Your heroine? Eleanor mouthed silently to me.

I smiled, for Miss Morland certainly had all the hallmarks of a heroine. She was sweet and innocent and honest and loving. She had a great affection for her brother. She was, for the present at least, without a mother, and under the care of her mother's friend. And if she was not presently threatened by some cruel marquis, well, she was young and there was still time!

Mistaking my silence for disapproval, Miss Morland went on hesitantly, 'But you never read novels, I dare say?'

'Why not?' I asked.

'Because they are not clever enough for you – gentlemen read better books.'

'The person, be it gentleman or lady, who has not pleasure in a good novel, must be intolerably stupid,' I assured her. 'I have read all Mrs Radcliffe's works, and most of them with great pleasure. The *Mysteries of Udolpho*, when I had once begun it, I could not lay down again; I remember finishing it in two days – my hair standing on end the whole time.'

'Yes,' said Eleanor, 'and I remember that you undertook to read it aloud to me, and that when I was called away for only five minutes to answer a note, instead of waiting for me, you took the volume into the Hermitage Walk, and I was obliged to stay till you had finished it.'

'Thank you, Eleanor – a most honourable testimony. You see, Miss Morland, the injustice of your suspicions. Here was I, in my eagerness to get on, refusing to wait only five minutes for my sister, breaking the promise I had made of reading it aloud, and keeping her in suspense at a most interesting part, by running away with the volume, which, you are to observe, was her own, particularly her own. I am proud when I reflect on it, and I think it must establish me in your good opinion.'

'I am very glad to hear it indeed, and now I shall never be ashamed of liking *Udolpho* myself. But I really thought before, young men despised novels amazingly,' said Miss Morland.

I assured her I had read dozens and laughed when she called

Udolpho 'nice'. Eleanor upbraided me for my impertinence, saying to Miss Morland, 'He is treating you exactly as he does his sister.'

And she was right. I was talking to Miss Morland with the ease that comes of friendship, instead of with the strained politeness that is usually necessary in Bath.

'I am sure I did not mean to say anything wrong,' said Miss Morland. 'But it is a nice book, and why should not I call it so?'

'Very true,' I said with a smile, 'and this is a very nice day, and we are taking a very nice walk, and you are two very nice young ladies. Oh! It is a very nice word indeed! It does for everything. Originally perhaps it was applied only to express neatness, propriety, delicacy, or refinement – people were nice in their dress, in their sentiments, or their choice. But now every commendation on every subject is comprised in that one word.'

'While, in fact,' said Eleanor, 'it ought only to be applied to you, without any commendation at all. You are more nice than wise. Come, Miss Morland, let us leave him to meditate over our faults in the utmost propriety of diction, while we praise *Udolpho* in whatever terms we like best. It is a most interesting work. You are fond of that kind of reading?'

'To say the truth, I do not much like any other.'

I laughed. There were many people who, I am sure, felt exactly as she did, but very few who had the courage to say so.

In the next half-hour I learned that she did not like history – 'it tells me nothing that does not either vex or weary me. The quarrels of popes and kings, with wars or pestilences, in every page; the men all so good for nothing, and hardly any women at all' – and was astonished when I admitted I was fond of it.

I discovered that she thought it was a torment for little children to learn to read – 'if you had been as much used as myself to hear poor little children first learning their letters and then learning to spell, if you had ever seen how stupid they can be for a whole morning together, and how tired my poor mother is at the end of it, as I am in the habit of seeing almost every day of my life at home, you would allow that "to torment" and "to instruct" might sometimes be used as synonymous words' – but she admitted that it was worth while to be tormented for two or three years of one's life, for the sake of being able to read all the rest of it.

'Consider, if reading had not been taught, Mrs Radcliffe would have written in vain, or perhaps might not have written at all,' I said.

'That indeed would have been a dreadful thing, for I have spent many happy hours with her books. It is a sad thought to even contemplate that she might never have written them. I begin to think as you do, that learning to read and write is no bad thing, after all. Her books are so very entertaining. And instructive, too. I am sure I know a great deal about Europe through reading her books; about France and the Alps and Italy. Why, without them I would know nothing of Venice at all. Do they really have gondolas to ride in?' she asked.

'Yes, they really do.'

'And is the city really full of canals?'

'Yes, it is.'

'Then I think that *Udolpho* is as good as a history book, and as instructive as any other, for though it does not contain as many facts, those facts it does contain are eagerly sought after and easily absorbed.'

'As good an argument for the studying of Mrs Radcliffe at Oxford as I have ever heard.'

We walked on, admiring the river and the line of the cliff.

As Eleanor and I discussed its suitability for a sketch, it was easy to see that Miss Morland had not had the benefit of a drawing master and I was happy to instruct her. I soon learnt that she had great natural taste, for when I pointed out the desirability of a drawing having the river in the foreground, with the rolling hills in the distance and a beech tree in the middle distance for perspective, she agreed with everything I said.

Talk of the oak led us to forests, forests to enclosures, enclosures to waste land, and from there it was a short step to politics, which is a subject likely to end any conversation. And so it was with this one.

After a while, Miss Morland recovered from politics and returned to her favourite theme, saying, 'I have heard that something very shocking indeed will soon come out in London. It is to be uncommonly dreadful. I shall expect murder and everything of the kind.'

Eleanor was alarmed, and Miss Morland was puzzled, and I laughed at them both.

'You talked of expected horrors in London,' I said, 'and instead of instantly conceiving, as any rational creature would have done, that such words could relate only to a circulating library, my sister immediately pictured to herself a mob of three thousand men assembling in St. George's fields, the Bank attacked, the Tower threatened, the streets of London flowing with blood, a detachment of the Twelfth Light Dragoons (the hopes of the nation) called up from Northampton to quell the insurgents, and the gallant Captain Frederick Tilney, in the moment of charging at the head of his troop, knocked off his horse by a brickbat from an upper window. Forgive her stupidity. The fears of the sister have added to the weakness of the woman; but she is by no means a simpleton in general.'

Eleanor laughed but Miss Morland, unsure whether I were serious or not, looked grave.

'And now, Henry, that you have made us understand each other, you may as well make Miss Morland understand yourself, unless you mean to have her think you intolerably rude to your sister, and a great brute in your opinion of women in general. Miss Morland is not used to your odd ways,' Eleanor said.

I smiled at Miss Morland's expression as understanding dawned, for she was no doubt realizing that Eleanor and I teased each other in the way that she and her brothers and sisters did.

'I shall be most happy to make her better acquainted with them,' I said.

My eyes lingered on her face. It really was remarkably pretty, surrounded by soft hair, and I thought that Miss Morland herself would be a fitting subject for a drawing.

'No doubt; but that is no explanation of the present,' said Eleanor.

'What am I to do?' I asked.

'You know what you ought to do. Clear your character handsomely before her. Tell her that you think very highly of the understanding of women.'

'Miss Morland, I think very highly of the understanding of all the women in the world, especially of those – whoever they may be – with whom I happen to be in company.'

'That is not enough. Be more serious.'

'Miss Morland, no one can think more highly of the understanding of women than I do. In my opinion, nature has given them so much that they never find it necessary to use more than half.'

Miss Morland looked perplexed, and I thought how well it became her.

'We shall get nothing more serious from him now, Miss Morland,' said Eleanor. 'He is not in a sober mood. But I do assure you that he must be entirely misunderstood, if he can ever appear to say an unjust thing of any woman at all, or an unkind one of me.'

Miss Morland smiled at me. I offered her my arm and as she took it I felt a surprising pleasure at her touch, and we continued with our walk.

Eleanor was not eager to lose Miss Morland's company, and neither was I. We accompanied her into the house in Pulteney Street where she was residing, and paid our respects to the Allens and then we parted, well pleased with each other.

'It seems you have found an agreeable friend,' I said to Eleanor. 'And, moreover, one my father is disposed to like.'

'And who would not like her? She is pretty, original, and becomingly ignorant,' said Eleanor.

I looked at her in surprise.

'Confess it! You loved instructing her,' said Eleanor.

'Instructing her? Nay, we were having an interesting conversation.'

'Interesting because you did most of the talking!'

'I happened to know the most about the subject, and besides, I always enjoy talking about art.'

'Of course, that is the reason and nothing else. Having a pretty young woman hanging on your every word and looking at you with awe has nothing to do with it.'

'Nothing at all!'

'Then you are a great deal nobler than the rest of your sex,' she said with a smile.

'I have often noticed it.'

'Be serious!'

'Well, then, you be serious,' I replied. 'I will agree with you that, to the larger and more trifling part of my sex, imbecility in females is a great enhancement of their personal charms; but I will point out that the remaining small portion of them are too reasonable and too well informed themselves to desire anything more in woman than ignorance.'

She laughed.

'And which kind are you?' she asked.

'I am my own kind; I am one of a kind. I require neither imbecility nor ignorance. Let a woman only be pretty, charming, kind to small animals and a lover of novels, and I am content.'

'Miss Morland manages the first three; only time will tell if she continues to manage the fourth!'

We went into our lodgings and as we went up to the drawing room I said, 'In all seriousness, I like Miss Morland.'

'In all seriousness,' said Eleanor, 'so do I. And that is fortunate, for with my father's approval, it seems we are destined to see much more of her.'

Tuesday 5 March

Having some business at the farrier's, what was my surprise to see Frederick there.

'I thought you were not coming to Bath until tomorrow,' I said.

'That is what I told our father but I arrived yesterday. I was determined to have some time to myself before I enjoyed his paternal affection,' he replied.

His eyes wandered from me to something over my shoulder and he gave a sneer.

'Now there goes a happy man,' he said.

I turned round to see Miss Morland's brother rushing past.

'He is on his way to Wiltshire to see his parents and ask for their consent to his marriage. He was in here not ten minutes ago with one of his friends, talking excitedly about it. The fair lady has accepted him, he is beloved by all her family, he is the special friend of her brother – all he needs is the approval of his father and he will willingly slip the noose around his own neck.'

I opened my mouth and then closed it again.

'What, little brother, no objection to make? That is not like you. You usually remonstrate with me when you hear me slighting the noble institution of matrimony. Have you begun to see the error of your ways?'

'In general, no,' I said.

'But in this case?'

'Let us just say, I do not envy him his choice of bride.'

'Ah! So that is it. Well, we will not repine. I dare say he is a fool and not worth our regrets,' said Frederick with a shrug.

'He is, from what I know of him, perfectly amiable, and the brother of a friend of mine.'

Something in my voice must have caught his attention for he said, 'A friend?' And looked at me penetratingly.

I had no wish to discuss Miss Morland with him and so I changed the subject, saying, 'Have you repaid Mr Morris what you owe him yet?'

'Morris?' asked Frederick.

'Yes. Thomas Morris, the man you invited to the abbey because you could not pay him what you owed him last autumn.'

'Ah, Morris. No, I have not paid him yet,' he said.

'Then you must hurry up and do so.'

'And why must I do so?' said Frederick provokingly.

'Because Eleanor is in love with him,' I replied.

'Eleanor? In love? I did not know she was in love with anyone, let alone Morris,' he said in surprise. 'I never noticed anything of it.'

'I assure you it is the case, and he is in love with her. So you see you must pay your debt. And no, it is no use your protesting that you cannot afford it, you have your allowance,' I reminded him.

'It will not make any difference. Our father will never give him permission, you know that as well as I. The general is eager for Eleanor to make a grand marriage, and if she cannot attract an earl or a viscount, or failing that a man with fifteen thousand a year, then he will marry her off to a relative of one of his cronies. I only wonder that he has not found some friend with a single relative for you.'

'He has often tried to do so. I am more surprised that he has not found someone for you. He is not happy with you, you know. He expected you to have risen beyond the rank of captain by now.'

'That is the trouble with having a general for a father, he expects me to reach the same exalted rank, but I have very little interest in soldiering. If I can drink in the mess room and wear a fine coat I am satisfied.'

'It may satisfy you, but it will not satisfy him, so have a care when you next see him to sound more enthusiastic, or he will stop your allowance.'

'I wish I did not have to see him at all,' said Frederick grimly. 'But enough of the general. I am meeting some friends at a tavern outside town. Come with me.'

'No, I thank you, I am meeting Charles in half an hour and must away.'

'Then I will see you tomorrow.'

He looked at me quizzically.

'Have no fear, I will not tell our father you have arrived.'

He nodded in thanks and I watched him go out of the farrier's, drawing admiring glances from a family of young ladies walking past. And then I was on my way, meeting Charles and riding on the hills and talking of his plans to return to his old neighbourhood.

'Bath is all very well,' he said, 'and when Margaret's family were alive we were settled here, but now that they have gone we are thinking of returning to the country. I want the children to have more space to run about and indulge in country pursuits. What do you think of the idea?'

'You will always be very welcome to us, you know that. I think it an excellent idea.'

'Good. We are thinking of looking for somewhere in the summer.'

Margaret was less enthusiastic, having lived in Bath all her life, but over dinner she warmed to the idea.

'I do not say it will be a bad thing,' she remarked, 'just that I will have to become accustomed to it. I would like the children to have more space to play, too, and I confess I would like to ride more, but I must insist we return to Bath each February. It is such a dull time in the country, but here there are the theatres and shops and concerts to brighten the month.'

Charles was agreeable, and being happily circumstanced, it was not impossible for him to promise it.

Theirs is a happy marriage and I wish Frederick could see it, but he seems to avoid his old friends and I fear he will refuse them. It is as if he does not want to let go of his ideas, for if he does he will have to throw himself once more back into life, heart and all, and risk having it broken all over again.

Wednesday 6 March

We were a subdued party at dinner tonight. It should have been a cheerful occasion, for Miss Morland joined us, but she brought with her the news that her brother is engaged to Isabella Thorpe, and that was not uplifting. Even worse was my father's overbearing manner, which cast a pall over everything.

Eleanor had a further reason for being quiet. I had told her that Frederick meant to pay Mr Morris back, but instead of pleasing her the news reminded her of what she had lost. It was left to my father, therefore, to entertain Miss Morland.

He must be serious about encouraging a friend for Eleanor for I can see no other reason why he would flatter Miss Morland so. But I am happy that he is pleased with her. The more I see of her, the more I am pleased with her myself, and I am looking forward to seeing her again tomorrow.

Thursday 7 March

Frederick arrived at Milsom Street this afternoon and was resolutely interrogated by my father as to his activities during his absence.

Having answered all my father's questions about his companions, his drinking habits and his spending, Frederick managed to lead the subject by degrees to the war. He engaged my father in a discussion of strategies and tactics for dealing with the French until it was time for us to leave for the Assembly Rooms.

My spirits were lifted by the presence of Miss Morland and I determined to make it up to her for the dullness of last night's party. I was soon laughing with her and teasing her and enjoying myself.

I enjoyed myself even more when she noticed Frederick, for although she evidently admired him – as who would not? – she did nothing to attract him, as other women have always done. This roused my admiration so much that I said I had a mind to dance and I was just about to ask her when Frederick laughed at me for finding it possible.

'In the Assembly Rooms? In Bath?' he mocked. 'You would not find me dancing here.'

'Then it is lucky I am not you. Miss Morland, would you do me the honour?' I asked.

Miss Morland, with a becoming smile, accepted.

The conversation soon turned to the outing she had missed in order to honour her engagement with Eleanor and myself.

'Did your friends put it off until you could join them?' I asked her.

'Oh, no, they went on their own; that is, Mr Thorpe drove his sister in my place.'

'That was not well done of him,' I said, 'but you seem to have survived the disappointment.'

'There was no disappointment at all, I assure you, although I thought they meant to go to Blaize Castle, and that I would have liked to see.'

'It is a fine old place.'

'You have been?' she asked me eagerly.

'On more than one occasion.'

'And is it very ancient?'

'Quite as ancient as you could wish, and quite as terrible. The venerable stones speak of all sorts of horrible incidents in its terrible past. Many a heroine has been forced into a travelling chaise and four and found herself transported to the castle, where she has been incarcerated, there to await her doom: marriage to an evil baron who will steal her fortune and then murder her, throwing her body into the deep limestone gorge that forms a dramatic backdrop to the castle.'

Her eyes sparkled.

'Do you really think so?' she asked with a pleasurable shiver.

'My dear Miss Morland, I am sure of it. Why, the folly alone has seen a dozen murders,' I remarked.

She looked momentarily disconcerted.

'But I thought it was only built some thirty or forty years ago,' she said.

'But where was it built? On the ruin of St Blaize's Chapel,' I said in a doleful voice.

'How perfectly horrid,' she said with delight.

'Yes, is it not? And to think, you were willing to forgo it in order to take a walk with Eleanor and myself. We cannot thank you enough for such a sacrifice.'

'It was not such a sacrifice,' she said artlessly, 'for they did not go to the castle in the end. I asked Isabella all about it. They merely drove to the York Hotel, where they ate some soup, and then walked down to the Pump-room, and after tasting the waters they ate an ice at a pastry-cook's, and then had to hurry back to the hotel and swallow their dinner in haste, to prevent being home in the dark.'

'Very well, you missed nothing of any interest, I grant you, but you did not know that at the time, and your sacrifice is no less noble,' I said.

At the end of the first dance, Frederick pulled me aside.

'You seem very taken with Miss Morland,' he said.

'I find her charming.'

'Who are her family?'

'No one in particular. She is here with neighbours, a Mr and Mrs Allen, and her brother is also here. He is the young man you saw at the farrier's. You will be delighted to know that his parents gave their consent to the match and he is now betrothed.'

'Lucky man,' said Frederick wryly.

His gaze had lingered on Miss Morland and when she looked up he caught her eye, but failing to win a smile or a flirtatious glance, his attention passed on to her friend. Miss Thorpe looked very pretty and was obviously longing to dance.

'There is someone I would like to know better. We collided when I was in pursuit of a drink and the experience was most agreeable. Introduce me,' said Frederick.

'Nay, Miss Thorpe is engaged, indeed she is engaged to Miss Morland's brother.'

'Is she indeed?' said Frederick with interest. 'And where is the happy Mr Morland?'

'He is still in Wiltshire, where he is no doubt discussing details of the marriage settlement with his parents.'

Frederick did not take his eyes from Miss Thorpe.

'What mischief are you planning?' I asked him.

'My dear little brother, how mistrustful you are. I? Mischief? For once in my life I am behaving myself, and doing my duty. There is a young lady in the room with no partner, and it is my concern, as a gentleman, to offer her my hand. You are dancing with her friend. Ask her if she thinks Miss Thorpe would like to dance.'

I was unwilling, but knowing Isabella Thorpe to be no innocent, and knowing that my brother could do her no harm in the assembly rooms, I did as he wished; that is, I asked Miss Morland if she though Miss Thorpe would have any objection to dancing.

'My brother would be most happy to be introduced to her,' I said.

'I am very sure Miss Thorpe does not mean to dance at all,' said Miss Morland.

I returned to Frederick with the news, and he appeared to accept it, for he walked away, but not two minutes later I saw him talking to Mrs Hughes and guessed that he would ask her for the introduction he had not received from me.

'Your brother will not mind it, I know,' said Miss Morland, knowing nothing of Frederick and assuming he was as generous and innocent as herself, 'because I heard him say before that he would never dance here; but it was very good-natured in him to think of it. I suppose he saw Isabella sitting down, and fancied she might wish for a partner; but he is quite mistaken, for she would not dance upon any account in the world.'

How is it possible for anyone to be so innocent and so charming?

I smiled, and said, 'How very little trouble it can give you to understand the motive of other people's actions.'

'Why? What do you mean?'

'With you, it is not: How is such a one likely to be influenced, What is the inducement most likely to act upon such a person's feelings, age, situation, and probable habits of life considered, but: How should I be influenced, What would be my inducement in acting so and so?'

'I do not understand you.'

'Then we are on very unequal terms, for I understand you perfectly well,' I said.

Honest, good-natured, artless and – for she likes me – intelligent! And also unwittingly funny, for she replied, 'Me? Yes; I cannot speak well enough to be unintelligible.'

I laughed.

'Bravo! An excellent satire on modern language,' I returned, pleased.

She was perplexed, which made her look even more enchanting.

'But pray tell me what you mean,' she said.

'Shall I indeed? Do you really desire it? But you are not aware of the consequences; it will involve you in a very cruel embarrassment, and certainly bring on a disagreement between us.'

'No, no; it shall not do either; I am not afraid,' she returned.

'Well, then, I only meant that your attributing my brother's wish of dancing with Miss Thorpe to good nature alone convinced me of your being superior in good nature yourself to all the rest of the world.'

She blushed and disclaimed, and the peach flush suffusing her cheeks made her eyes look even more bright.

Her blushes and smiles subsided, however, when she happened to glance to her right and saw Miss Thorpe standing up with my brother. She was astonished; I, alas, was not at all surprised. Frederick had decided to seduce Miss Thorpe and there was not anything I could do to stop him. The only person who could stop him now was Miss Thorpe herself.

If she had been defenceless I would have stepped in, but she was in Bath with her family, and engaged to a good and honest man. And so I let him have his way, knowing that she had plenty of people to look after her, and that one word from her own lips would send Frederick on his way. For although he is a rake he is not cruel, and has never yet seduced a woman too young or friendless to be able to resist his charms.

Miss Thorpe, seeing herself observed, shrugged her shoulders and smiled, the only explanation of this extraordinary change which could at that time be given; but as it was not quite enough for Miss Morland's comprehension, she spoke her astonishment in very plain terms to me: 'I cannot think how it could happen! Isabella was so determined not to dance.'

'And did Isabella never change her mind before?' I asked.

'Oh! But, because – And your brother! After what you told him from me, how could he think of going to ask her?'

'I cannot take surprise to myself on that head. You bid me be surprised on your friend's account, and therefore I am; but as for my brother, his conduct in the business, I must own, has been no more than I believed him perfectly equal to. The fairness of your friend was an open attraction; her firmness, you know, could only be understood by yourself.'

'You are laughing; but, I assure you, Isabella is very firm in general.'

'It is as much as should be said of anyone. To be always firm must be to be often obstinate. When properly to relax is the trial of judgment; and, without reference to my brother, I really think Miss Thorpe has by no means chosen ill in fixing on the present hour.'

The dance over, Miss Morland was claimed by her friend, and they walked about the room arm in arm, with Miss Thorpe no doubt explaining why she had broken her steadfast resolve of not dancing, and Miss Morland being surprised and yet generous enough to believe whatever her friend cared to tell her.

Monday 11 March

Just as I thought we were settled in Bath, my father announced at breakfast that we would be returning to the abbey on Saturday se'ennight. A couple of letters were the cause of his change of plan: one from his steward, saying that his presence was needed at home and one from General Courteney, saying that he and the Marquis of Longtown had been unavoidably delayed and would not be coming to Bath after all.

Eleanor breathed a sigh of relief that the general and the marquis would not be joining us, but she was as disappointed as I was to be leaving Bath until my father said, 'You must invite your friend to come with us, Eleanor. I am sure she would like to see the abbey and it will be company for you, you know.'

I was surprised, not sorry for the suggestion and neither was Eleanor.

My father set out immediately to ask the Allens for their consent to the scheme and I asked Eleanor if she knew of any reason why our father has singled out Miss Morland, more than any of the other young ladies of our acquaintance.

'I like her very well, and so do you,' I mused, 'but our father is disposed to dislike people in general, and I see nothing in Miss Morland which would impress him.'

'Except perhaps for her sweetness and her willingness to please and be pleased,' said Eleanor. 'I hope she accepts our invitation but I fear she might not want to leave her brother. I am sorry for him, engaging himself to Miss Thorpe. She is not good enough for him.'

'No, far from it, but she is pretty, lively and flirtatious, and he is not the first young man to lose his head over such a one as Miss Thorpe.'

'Frederick seems interested in her, too.'

'Frederick is interested in her only because he cannot have her; unless he has some mischief planned,' I remarked. 'However, Miss Thorpe knows what she is about. She will have to look out for herself. It is Miss Morland in whom I have an interest, and so, too, for some reason, does our father.'

'Perhaps it is just that he noticed I have a liking for her.'

'I think it must be, for I can think of no other reason. And so she is to visit us at the abbey?'

'I have not asked her yet. She might say no.'

'What? Say no to staying in a real abbey?' I enquired. 'No lover of Gothic novels could resist.'

'You must promise me not to tell her it is haunted. I think she might believe you, and I would not have her frightened.'

'Frightened? My dear Eleanor, if she saw a ghost in the abbey it would delight her for the rest of her life. A headless horseman or a spectral woman wringing her hands, or some ill-fated nun, would thrill her to the core.'

She smiled.

'I suppose it would. Very well, you may tease her if you will.'

Miss Morland arrived at that moment and my father returned soon after. He added his entreaties to Eleanor's and Miss Morland was very quickly persuaded to accept the invitation, as long as her parents gave their consent.

She returned to the Allens happily, leaving Eleanor and myself scarcely any less happy with the promise of her company.

Tuesday 12 March

Our change of plan has necessitated a change in my arrangements. I called on the Plainters to let them know that I will not be able to dine with them on the twenty-fifth and as they were just about to set out for a drive with a party of friends they persuaded me to go with them. I knew some of the party but there were some I did not know and some I wished I did not know. Miss Smith was there, as scathing as ever about her fellows; barbed comments delivered with humour I can enjoy but not those without. Miss Crane was also there, shy and demure. I tried to laugh her out of it, for, like Miss Morland, she is fresh from the country, but she would not even smile. I asked her about her hobbies – she has none; her favourite books – she does not read; the assemblies – she has no opinion. I relinquished her with gratitude to Margaret and found myself the object of Miss Brown's attention. Miss Brown said she was not surprised we were leaving, for Bath had nothing to offer: the assemblies were dull, the people without taste and the concerts not worth listening to. I confounded her by saying that I liked the place and was only sorry not to be staying longer.

'Well, and do any of the ladies take your fancy?' asked Charles as we reached our destination and waited for the rest of the party to dismount or climb out of the carriages.

'Alas, no.'

'I thought at one time you were partial to Miss Morland but I hear she is to marry Thorpe,' he said, as he threw the reins of his horse over a branch.

I was astonished.

'Do you indeed?' I said.

'Yes. I had it from Thorpe himself. He tried to sell me a horse and when he saw he could not sell it to me for myself he tried to sell it to me for Margaret, remarking that he had intended to give it to his betrothed but that Miss Morland did not happen to like bay.'

'But is it certain?' I asked. 'It seems a strange match to me.' Thinking: And a highly unlikely one.

'Thorpe seems to think so. His sister marrying Miss Morland's brother gave him the idea and Miss Morland apparently agreed.'

Margaret had by this time joined us and remarked, 'I should be very surprised if Miss Morland thinks herself engaged. There has been no announcement and from what I can gather, the proposal was hardly conventional: Mr Thorpe said that marriage was a good thing and when Miss Morland agreed he took it as a "yes" to a question he does not appear to have asked.'

'That seems more likely,' I said, 'for whenever I have seen them together she seemed to regard him with aversion.'

'I regard him the same way myself,' said Charles. 'He has no interest in anyone but himself and tells the most preposterous stories about his exploits. To hear him talk, anyone would think he was the best swimmer, rider, billiard-player, boxer, hunter and everything else the world has ever seen.'

'Charles would not let me invite him today, even though we were short of gentlemen,' said Margaret.

'Ah, so that is why you invited me,' I said.

'Of course,' said Charles with a laugh. 'Why else?'

'And, being short of gentlemen, you would very much oblige me if you would escort Mrs Redbridge and her daughter to the top of the hill. They are waiting for a gentleman's arm.'

I viewed the Redbridges with some misgivings, for their faces wore an assessing look, as though they were measuring everything from the capes on my greatcoat to the value of my tithes. But I did my duty and was rewarded by a fine spread eaten in the sharp March wind, before persistent rain broke up the party and returned us all to Bath.

What was my pleasure to find Miss Morland in Milsom Street. As I entered the drawing room I heard her asking Eleanor, in excited tones, 'And was the abbey once a convent?'

'Yes, and a richly endowed one, until the Reformation,' said Eleanor. 'It then fell into the hands of one of our ancestors on its dissolution.'

'And is it very ancient?' asked Miss Morland breathlessly.

'Quite as ancient as you could wish. A large portion of the original building still makes a part of the present dwelling, although some has decayed.'

'And does it stand in a valley, surrounded by heavy trees?'

'Yes, if you call oak trees heavy.'

'I should think they are,' said Miss Morland with delight.

'Pray, do not let me interrupt,' I said as they looked up and saw me.

'I cannot believe I am to stay in a real abbey,' said Miss Morland.

'I only hope it does not disappoint you,' said Eleanor.

'Oh, no! I am sure it could never do that.'

The new fittings and sound masonry are perhaps not what she is expecting, nor are the neat gardens and the useful offices, but I am glad to be taking her away from the Thorpes and I mean to make sure she enjoys herself.

Wednesday 13 March

We were late arriving at the Pump-room and to my disappointment I learnt that Miss Morland, who had been there earlier with Mrs Allen, had already left. Her friend Miss Thorpe was there, however, busily flirting with Frederick. Eleanor and I both noticed, and we exchanged glances.

'Why do you think the fair Isabella is flirting with Frederick?' I asked her. 'Is it because her swain is absent and she is practising for his return?'

'Do you think that is the reason?' she said.

'No, alas. I think that Miss Thorpe is a hardened flirt, and I pity Morland from my heart.'

'For his sake or his sister's?'

'Both. He has done nothing to deserve this, save being wilfully blind and attributing perfection to the object of his affections and ignoring her feet of clay. But that is no more than the best of us will do in love, and he is to be pitied rather than blamed.'

'And have you attributed perfection to your favourite, instead of looking at her feet?'

'I have attributed nothing to Miss Morland that she does not already possess: charm – the kind that comes from within, which is seldom met with, and not the practised kind, which is to be found everywhere; originality, for there is nothing more original than speaking one's mind, without dissemble or disguise; and a love of Mrs Radcliffe, which is the most important of the three.'

'Do be serious, Henry,' she said with a smile.

'I was never more so.'

'Very well, then, have it your own way, a love of Mrs Radcliffe is the most important asset to happiness in a long life lived together.'

'A long life lived together? My dear sister, what are you thinking?'

'That you are destined for Miss Morland; or, perhaps I should say, that she is destined for you.'

'Poor Eleanor, you are sadly deceived. She is but one of my flirts.'

Eleanor laughed.

'Oh, no, Henry, you will have to do better than that. When I spoke of your favourite, you immediately assumed I was speaking of Miss Morland, not Miss Smith or Miss Crane or Miss Parsons, and why would you do that unless you favoured the lady above all others?'

'My dear Eleanor, you have found me out. I have tried very hard to love Miss Parsons, her name being so suitable for a clergyman's wife, but her tendency to flirt with every other man when my back is turned is decidedly against the plan.'

'Which brings us back to Miss Thorpe.'

I glanced again at Miss Thorpe, who was practically sitting on Frederick's knee, she was so close to him. His mouth was almost touching her ear, whispering, I am sure, the flattering nothings of which he is such a master.

'Is she tired of her betrothed already, or was there never much love there, do you think?' I asked.

'The latter, I think,' said Eleanor.

'Then why did she consent to marry him? I know that every young woman likes to be asked for her hand, it is a trophy for her to parade around all her friends, but unless she is particularly stupid she does not give it, not without love, or at the very least, a desire for a respectable establishment.'

'I am puzzled by that myself,' said Eleanor. 'Mr Morland has no money to tempt her—'

'Are you certain of that? If there is an unexpected fortune, then that might explain why my father is so fond of Miss Morland.'

'I am sure of it. I congratulated Miss Thorpe on her engagement and she poured out the facts: that, although money meant nothing to her and she would be glad to live on twenty pounds a year, her dear James had only a living of four hundred pounds a year, and that he must wait several years for even that. I fancy she mistook Morland's wealth and thought him rich.'

'It is always possible. She is certainly stupid enough, though his coat is as good an indication of his lack of wealth as a full disclosure of his expectations.'

'Perhaps she thought him merely negligent in his dress,' said Eleanor.

'Or allowed hope to overcome sense. Or merely thought it would be worth her while consenting to the engagement on the chance he might be well provided for, with the intention of looking elsewhere if such proved not to be the case.'

'Whatever the case, I fear she is making her acknowledged suitor very unhappy.'

Morland had now entered, and was looking uncomfortable as he approached her. Frederick, with a last whisper in Miss Thorpe's ear, drew back, and Morland was left to the half hearted attentions of his future bride, whose eyes too often sought out my brother.

Thursday 14 March

The Pump-rooms were quiet this morning but Miss Morland was there with the Allens and almost as soon as I had greeted her she said, 'Mr Tilney, I cannot bear to see your brother unhappy, or mine either, and I think there must have been some dreadful mistake. Miss Thorpe, you know, is engaged to my brother, and so she can never belong to Captain Tilney. Her spirits are unguarded and her manner is lively, and I think she might have unconsciously led your brother to believe that her heart was free, and that his attentions were welcome; even worse, that they were returned. I would not like to see him suffer, so I beg you will let him know that Miss Thorpe is engaged to my brother, allowing him to withdraw with dignity.'

'But my brother does know it,' I replied.

'Does he? Then why does he stay here? For I heard him say that he does not intend to return to the abbey with you, and that instead he intends to remain in Bath.'

It was a difficult question to answer and, to give myself time to think, I began to talk of something else; but she eagerly continued, 'Why do not you persuade him to go away? The longer he stays, the worse it will be for him at last. Pray advise him for his own sake, and for everybody's sake, to leave Bath directly. Absence will in time make him comfortable again; but he can have no hope here, and it is only staying to be miserable.'

I smiled at that, I could not help it, and remarked, 'I am sure my brother would not wish to do that.'

'Then you will persuade him to go away?' she beseeched me.

'Persuasion is not at command; but pardon me, if I cannot even endeavour to persuade him. I have myself told him that Miss Thorpe is engaged. He knows what he is about, and must be his own master.'

'No, he does not know what he is about,' cried Catherine. 'He does not know the pain he is giving my brother. Not that James has ever told me so, but I am sure he is very uncomfortable.'

'And are you sure it is my brother's doing?'

'Yes, very sure.'

'Is it my brother's attentions to Miss Thorpe, or Miss Thorpe's admission of them, that gives the pain?' I asked, hoping to open her eyes to the reality of her friend's true nature, but in such away that it would not give her too much pain.

'Is not it the same thing?' she asked, confused.

'I think Mr Morland would acknowledge a difference. No man is offended by another man's admiration of the woman he loves; it is the woman only who can make it a torment.'

She blushed for her friend, and said, 'Isabella is wrong. But I am sure she cannot mean to torment, for she is very much attached to my brother. She has been in love with him ever since they first met, and while my father's consent was uncertain, she fretted herself almost into a fever. You know she must be attached to him.'

'I understand,' I said. 'She is in love with James, and flirts with Frederick.'

'Oh! no, not flirts. A woman in love with one man cannot flirt with another.'

'It is probable that she will neither love so well, nor flirt so well, as she might do either singly. The gentlemen must each give up a little.'

After a short pause, she resumed with, 'Then you do not believe Isabella so very much attached to my brother?'

She spoke hesitantly, but I was glad that her eyes were opening.

'I can have no opinion on that subject,' I remarked.

'But what can your brother mean? If he knows her engagement, what can he mean by his behaviour?'

'You are a very close questioner,' I said.

'Am I? I only ask what I want to be told,' she said.

'But do you only ask what I can be expected to tell?'

'Yes, I think so; for you must know your brother's heart.'

'My brother's heart, as you term it, on the present occasion, I assure you I can only guess at.'

'Well?'

'Well! Nay, if it is to be guesswork, let us all guess for ourselves. To be guided by second-hand conjecture is pitiful. The premises are before you. My brother is a lively and perhaps sometimes a thoughtless young man; he has had about a week's acquaintance with your friend, and he has known her engagement almost as long as he has known her.'

'Well,' said Catherine, after some moments' consideration, 'you may be able to guess at your brother's intentions from all this; but I am sure I cannot. But is not your father uncomfortable about it? Does not he want Captain Tilney to go away? Sure, if your father were to speak to him, he would go.'

'My dear Miss Morland,' I said, 'in this amiable solicitude for your brother's comfort, may you not be a little mistaken? Are you not carried a little too far? Would he thank you, either on his own account or Miss Thorpe's, for supposing that her affection, or at least her good behaviour, is only to be secured by her seeing nothing of Captain Tilney? Is he safe only in solitude? Or is her heart constant to him only when unsolicited by anyone else? He cannot think this, and you may be sure that he would not have you think it. I will not say, "Do not be uneasy", because I know that you are so, at this moment; but be as little uneasy as you can. You have no doubt of the mutual attachment of your brother and your friend; depend upon it, therefore, that real jealousy never can exist between them; depend upon it that no disagreement between them can be of any duration. Their hearts are open to each other, as neither heart can be to you; they know exactly what is required and what can be borne; and you may be certain that one will never tease the other beyond what is known to be pleasant.'

She still looked doubtful and grave, and so I added, 'Though Frederick does not leave Bath with us, he will probably remain but a very short time, perhaps only a few days behind us. His leave of absence will soon expire, and he must return to his regiment. And what will then be their acquaintance? The mess-room will drink Isabella Thorpe for a fortnight, and she will laugh with your brother over poor Tilney's passion for a month.'

She was comforted and I envied her, for I wished I could be comforted so easily; in short, I wished I knew what Frederick was thinking of. It is no use me asking him, he will not answer; and so I am glad we are to leave Bath and that he will soon quit the

place, too. After that, James Morland must take his chances with
the next handsome rogue who happens to come by.

Saturday 16 March

This morning I returned to the abbey to make sure that everything would be prepared in advance of our return next week. If
only my father had not been so vigorous in his renovations then
Miss Morland would be able to revel in a large and gloomy
chamber hung with tapestries, and a rug placed askew to reveal
the edge of a trapdoor; instead I can offer her nothing better than
the guest room, with papered walls and a carpeted floor, bright
windows and comfortable furniture and – worst of all – a cheerful
air.

Having given the housekeeper notice of our impending return
I rode over to Woodston. It was already dark by the time I
arrived, the days not yet being long enough to provide me with
an easy journey, but it was one I wanted to make so that I would
be able to preach tomorrow and to give my curate warning of my
intentions.

Though Bath has been very enjoyable – unexpectedly so – I
find I am glad to be home.

Sunday 17 March

An interesting service, attended by a full congregation and a large
complement of coughs and sneezes, so that I counted myself
fortunate if I managed to get out one sentence in ten without
interruption. Everything I have learnt about volume and diction
has come from other orators but in justice to myself I can say that
the art of timing my words to match the gaps in the assorted
barks and splutterings of a March congregation is all my own. I

believe I will write a paper on it, for I am sure it will be of use to more than myself.

After the service I was presented with the usual collection of pen-wipers, and believe I now have enough to last me the rest of my life.

Monday 18 March

Back to Bath, bearing a note for my sister which had arrived from Mr Morris. She took it upstairs and returned to the drawing room some time later with sparkling eyes that spoke of delights perused and perhaps a few tears shed, too. I am sorry for her. But if my father is prepared to encourage Miss Morland as a friend for her, then there is a chance that in time he will come to see Mr Morris as a possible match, for his attitudes on fortune seem to be mellowing. I hope so. Eleanor has never shown any interest in anyone before, though she has met plenty of young men; indeed, in the last few weeks in Bath she has danced with several dozen. But none of them has aroused her interest in the way that Morris has.

I found myself thinking that my mother would have liked him, for she had a romantic nature to contrast with my father's worldly air; and then I found myself thinking of their three children, who were a mixture of both, giving that curious blend of idealism coupled with cynicism that infects both Frederick and myself, he with more of the latter since his disappointment and me with more of the former. And Eleanor, hopeful like my mother, but also steeped in my father's realistic nature, dreaming of her Mr Morris but knowing that Papa will never consent to the match, unless a miracle should happen. And when did a miracle ever happen, except in the pages of a novel? What *deus ex machine* can save her from the unhappiness of disappointed love? What God, descending on a platform from the back of the stage, can relieve her heartache? Aphrodite, perhaps, to solve the lovers' obstacles? Ares, maybe, to give my father, the soldier, a change of heart? Or Minerva, goddess of wisdom, to show him the error of his ways.

Tuesday 19 March

Our father has changed the plans again, and we are now to leave Bath on Friday instead of Saturday. The Allens have been asked for their approval of the new day and have given it, so everything is now set for Friday.

Friday 22 March

Miss Morland joined us in Milsom Street for breakfast, as arranged. She was brought to us by Mr Allen. I was glad to see how carefully he watched over, and how he looked about him, to make sure that we were suitable people and that we would do everything in our power to make her stay with us a happy one.

My father was affability itself. Whether it was the thought of returning to the abbey, or whether the waters have really done him good, I do not know, but he was in good spirits and showed to great advantage. He was courteous in his welcome to Miss Morland, saying how grateful Eleanor was to have her company, and he was charming to Mr Allen, who brought Miss Morland to us.

'We cannot thank you enough for being willing to part with your fair friend,' he said to Mr Allen. 'We have seen how her company has brightened your stay in Bath, and we know that you must miss her when we take her away from you.'

'That we will,' said Mr Allen. 'Catherine's a good girl, and she has made my gout bearable, which is a thing I did not think possible. She is always cheerful and her good humour puts me in a good humour myself. Mrs Allen feels it as much as I do, we have been very glad to have her with us. But young people like to have other young people about them, and we are pleased that she has made such a good friend in Miss Tilney. We will only be in Bath for one more week ourselves and then we will be returning to Fullerton.'

'We know how important you are in that neighbourhood. Bath's loss is Fullerton's gain,' said my father.

Mr Allen bowed. Then, having satisfied himself that Miss Morland was amongst friends and that she would be well cared for, he said goodbye and took his leave.

'And now we have you all to ourselves,' said my father to Miss Morland. 'We have prepared a small repast, nothing such as you are used to, but a simple meal to set us on our way.'

He led the way into the dining room, where breakfast was set out and where we were, belatedly, joined by Frederick. My father continued to frighten Miss Morland with his deference, in between annoying Frederick by his lectures and worrying Eleanor because she could see that his exaggerated courtesy was making us late. He would not hurry Miss Morland, however, and kept pressing her to eat, so that we did not leave the table until a quarter to ten, and the clock was striking the hour when the trunks were at last carried down to the carriages.

'Ten o'clock! We should be away!' he said.

But we were not, and the delays continued whilst he found fault with the seating arrangements in the chaise, giving the maid instructions to move some of the parcels, so that Miss Morland was only just able to prevent him from throwing her writing table out by mistake.

At last, however, the door was closed upon the three females, and they set off, with my father and myself following in my curricle. We stopped for lunch at Petty France, where my father berated the waiters, complained abut the postilion, and generally made us all uncomfortable, so that scarcely anything was said but by himself. However, he then had a happy thought, and said, 'The day is fine, and I am anxious for you seeing as much of the country as possible, Miss Morland. Why do you not take my place in the curricle and I will travel with my daughter? You need not have any fear that Henry will overset you. He is a very good driver.'

Miss Morland blushed, but it was soon arranged, and she was sitting in the curricle beside me, beaming with delight.

'I believe we could have been ready in half the time, had we all travelled by curricle,' said Miss Morland, as we left the inn. 'The chaise is very grand, to be sure, but it took a deal of time to ready for the onward journey. I do believe we could pass the chaise in half a minute, if your father was not disposed to travel in front.'

'Then if you like travelling in it so well, I must take you out often,' I said. 'It is the least I can do to thank you for your kindness to Eleanor. It is a sign of real friendship, and I assure you that both Eleanor and I are grateful for it. Eleanor is uncomfortably circumstanced at the Abbey. She has no female companion, and in the frequent absences of my father, she is sometimes without any companion at all.'

'But how can that be?' she asked. 'Are not you with her?'

I explained that Northanger was not more than half my home and that I had an establishment at my own house in Woodston.

'How sorry you must be for that!' she said.

'I am always sorry to leave Eleanor.'

'Yes; but besides your affection for her, you must be so fond of the abbey! After being used to such a home as the abbey, an ordinary parsonage house must be very disagreeable.'

I smiled and said that she had formed a very favourable idea of the abbey.

'To be sure, I have. Is not it a fine old place, just like what one reads about?'

'And are you prepared to encounter all the horrors that a building such as "what one reads about" may produce? Have you a stout heart? Nerves fit for sliding panels and tapestry?' I asked.

'Oh! yes,' she said in breathless delight. 'I do not think I should be easily frightened, because there would be so many people in the house, and besides, it has never been uninhabited and left deserted for years, and then the family come back to it unawares, without giving any notice, as generally happens.'

'No, certainly. I came back myself last week to give the housekeeper notice of our return. We shall not have to explore our way into a hall dimly lighted by the expiring embers of a wood fire, nor be obliged to spread our beds on the floor of a room without windows, doors, or furniture. But you must be aware that when a young lady is (by whatever means) introduced into a dwelling of this kind, she is always lodged apart from the rest of the family. While they snugly repair to their own end of the house, she is formally conducted by Dorothy, the ancient housekeeper, up a different staircase, and along many gloomy passages, into an apartment never used since some cousin or kin died in it about twenty years before. Can you stand such a ceremony as this? Will not your mind misgive you when you find yourself in this gloomy chamber, too lofty and extensive for you, with only the feeble rays of a single lamp to take in its size, its walls hung with tapestry exhibiting figures as large as life, and the bed, of dark-green stuff or purple velvet, presenting even a funereal appearance? Will not your heart sink within you?'

'Oh! But this will not happen to me, I am sure,' she said.

'How fearfully will you examine the furniture of your apartment! And what will you discern? Not tables, toilettes, wardrobes, or drawers, but on one side perhaps the remains of a broken lute, on the other a ponderous chest which no efforts can open, and over the fireplace the portrait of some handsome warrior, whose features will so incomprehensibly strike you, that you will not be able to withdraw your eyes from it. Dorothy, meanwhile, no less struck by your appearance, gazes on you in great agitation, and drops a few unintelligible hints. To raise your spirits, moreover, she gives you reason to suppose that the part of the abbey you inhabit is undoubtedly haunted, and informs you that you will not have a single domestic within call. With this parting cordial she curtsies off, you listen to the sound of her receding footsteps as long as the last echo can reach you. And when, with fainting spirits, you attempt to fasten your door, you discover, with increased alarm, that it has no lock.'

Her eyes were wide, and she gave a pleasurable shiver.

'Oh! Mr Tilney, how frightful! This is just like a book! But it cannot really happen to me. I am sure your housekeeper is not really Dorothy. Well, what then?'

'Nothing further to alarm perhaps may occur the first night. After surmounting your unconquerable horror of the bed, you will retire to rest, and get a few hours' unquiet slumber. But on the second, or at farthest the third night after your arrival, you will probably have a violent storm. Peals of thunder so loud as to seem to shake the edifice to its foundation will roll round the neighbouring mountains, and during the frightful gusts of wind which accompany it, you will probably think you discern (for your lamp is not extinguished) one part of the hanging more violently agitated than the rest. Unable of course to repress your curiosity in so favourable a moment for indulging it, you will instantly arise, and throwing your dressing-gown around you, proceed to examine this mystery. After a very short search, you will discover a division in the tapestry so artfully constructed as to defy all but the minutest inspection, and on opening it, a door will immediately appear – which door, being only secured by massy bars and a padlock, you will, after a few efforts, succeed in opening and, with your lamp in your hand, will pass through it into a small vaulted room.'

'No, indeed; I should be too much frightened to do any such thing.'

'What! Not when Dorothy has given you to understand that there is a secret subterraneous communication between your apartment and the chapel of St Anthony, scarcely two miles off? Could you shrink from so simple an adventure? No, no, you will proceed into this small vaulted room, and through this into several others, without perceiving anything very remarkable in either. In one perhaps there may be a dagger, in another a few drops of blood, and in a third the remains of some instrument of torture; but there being nothing in all this out of the common way, and your lamp being nearly exhausted, you will return towards your own apartment. In repassing through the small vaulted room, however, your eyes will be attracted towards a large, old-fashioned cabinet of ebony and gold, which, though narrowly examining the furniture before, you had passed unnoticed. Impelled by an irresistible presentiment, you will eagerly advance to it, unlock its folding doors, and search into every drawer, but for some time without discovering anything of importance – perhaps nothing but a considerable hoard of diamonds. At last, however, by touching a secret spring, an inner compartment will open – a roll of paper appears – you seize it – it contains many sheets of manuscript – you hasten with the precious treasure into your own chamber, but scarcely have you been able to decipher "O Thou! – whomsoever thou mayst be, into whose hands these memoirs of the wretched Matilda may fall—" when your lamp suddenly expires in the socket, and leaves you in total darkness.'

'Oh! No, no, do not say so,' she said, all agog, and hanging on every word. 'Well, go on.'

But it was no good. I could not go on, I was too busy laughing.

'You will have to use your own imagination!' I said.

She came back from her horrid visions to reality and tried to pretend that she had not been carried away, and said she was sure that Eleanor would never put her in such a chamber. And then, to prove that she had never taken any of it seriously, she remarked on the fields and the country lanes, and talked of nothing but commonplaces until we drew near the abbey.

Upon my remarking that we were entering into the neigh-bourhood, however, her excitement began to grow. She looked ahead eagerly, craning her neck around corners in an effort to catch an early glimpse of it.

'We will be seeing it at any moment,' she said.

'No, not until we pass through the gates of the lodge,' I said. 'It sits very low to the ground and cannot be seen from any great distance.'

'We must surely see a chimney.'

Alas! I knew it was not the case but I did not like to disappoint her, and the final stages of the journey were passed by her in a state of pleasurable excitement which I found entrancing.

As we passed by the lodge I saw a look of surprise cross her face, for there is no denying it, the lodge has a modern appear-ance, and she was no less surprised by the well-kept drive, which allowed us to pass smoothly along it, instead of enveloping us in overhanging branches and mossy creepers.

The weather sprang to her aid, however, and a sudden scud of rain added a semblance of horror as we pulled up before the abbey, though the horror was only that it might ruin her new straw bonnet, instead of leading to a fearful presentiment that she would be abducted by *banditti* or harsh-voiced mercenaries.

I helped her down from the carriage, my hands closing about her waist with a satisfying feeling of pleasure. She was soon beneath the shelter of the old porch, and then passing into the hall, where Eleanor and my father were waiting to welcome her.

I watched with amusement as we went into the drawing room and she saw the modern furniture and the Rumford fireplace, with its slabs of marble instead of ponderous stone, and the pretty English china instead of two-handed axes and rusting shields.

My father, misunderstanding her air of disappointment, immediately began to apologize for the room, whilst taking out his watch, a habit of his, and saying with surprise, 'But it is within twenty minutes of five!'

Eleanor and I knew at once what that meant: it was time to dress for dinner. Eleanor hurried Miss Morland upstairs. I retired to my own room, amusing myself by imagining Miss Morland's feelings at being in a real abbey, with its broad staircases of shining oak, its wide galleries and its quadrangles; though these could be but a poor substitute for dungeons, cells and secret passages.

I was soon dressed, and met Eleanor on the landing as I was on my way down to dinner. She was walking there, looking anxious.

'Miss Morland has not yet come out of her room, and you know how Father is about punctuality,' she said in dismay.

'Then go in, and see if she is ready.'

'Yes, I think I must. I do not want to hurry her, but ...'

And so saying, she disappeared into Miss Morland's room. I went downstairs to find my father pacing the drawing room and looking at his pocket watch.

'Where are they?' he demanded irascibly.

'They will be here directly,' I said. 'Ladies, you know, take longer to dress than gentlemen.'

'It is a confounded nuisance,' he said, as though he had an appointment, when in fact there was no need whatsoever for dinner to be served at that minute, other than his love of running the house with the precision of a military campaign.

Eleanor and Miss Morland appeared a few minutes later. My father's irritation did not noticeably subside and he barked, 'Dinner to be on the table at once!' to the footman. He offered Miss Morland his arm and, leaving me to escort Eleanor, he went through to the dining room.

'I hope we are not to have this every night,' I said to Eleanor, thinking that Miss Morland looked frightened.

'I think Catherine will never dare be late again,' said Eleanor.

'You must send your maid to help her tomorrow night,' I said, 'for she has not brought one with her and it must be difficult for her to dress on her own.'

'I did, but she sent Annie away. She was busy examining her room when I went in, and small wonder, for it is all new to her. She was fascinated by the old chest. It is a curious object, I suppose—'

She looked at me curiously as I began to laugh.

'Depend upon it, she was thinking it hid some fiendish secret: a body, perhaps, or a mound of jewels!' I said.

Eleanor smiled and replied, 'Henry, no!'

'Why not? She is excited at being in an abbey, and she would not be a heroine if she did not entertain such a notion for a minute, at least.'

'Then she must have been sadly disappointed, for she found nothing but linen!' said Eleanor with a laugh. Then, more seriously, 'And is she a heroine?'

'She is most certainly that. But, I take it, you mean, is she my heroine?'

'Well?'

'As to that, I cannot say. I like her.' My eyes lingered on her as she took her place at table. 'Yes, I like her very much. But I have seen her very little as yet, you know. One can never know someone by dancing with them at assemblies and the like. Here, where I will see her day by day for the next few weeks, I will be able to see if the liking is just that, or anything more.'

'And she will be able to see you.'

'Also important,' I said. 'I want no unwilling bride, however much such creatures might amuse me in a novel; for whilst it is very pleasant to read about young ladies incarcerated in castles, with devious guardians and sinister suitors forcing them into horrible marriages, it is not so pleasant in real life. Then it is better to be surrounded by friends, and to laugh a great deal.'

There was time for no more. We took our places at table and the soup was immediately served.

'This is a very spacious room,' said Miss Morland, looking about her.

My father, recovering from his ill humour, for of all things he likes everything to be punctual, was all charm again.

'It is by no means an ill-sized room,' he said. 'Though I am as careless on such subjects as most people, I look upon a tolerably large eating-room as one of the necessaries of life; I suppose that you must have been used to much better-sized apartments at Mr Allen's?'

A suspicion took hold of me, as it had done before, that he had somehow mistaken her for an heiress, and that that was the cause of his charm. But upon Miss Morland's saying, 'No, indeed. Mr Allen's dining parlour is not more than half as large. I have never seen so large a room as this in my life,' he was not at all put out, as he surely must have been if he had thought of her as a wealthy young lady. Instead, his good humour increased, and I supposed that he liked having someone to whom he could show off.

'Why, as I have such rooms, it would be simple not to make use of them,' he said. 'But upon my honour, I believe there might be more comfort in rooms of only half their size. Mr Allen's house, I am sure, must be exactly of the true size for rational happiness. But tell me, Miss Morland, is your room to your liking?'

'Oh, yes, it is very grand,' she said. 'I have never seen a finer chamber.'

'There are no headless spectres?' I asked her innocently.

She blushed.

My father frowned and drew her attention back to the dinner. But when he had left us, called away by some letters he needed to answer, the mood grew lighter and I was able to tease her at my leisure. The night was stormy and the wind, which had been rising at intervals the whole afternoon, was heard to moan on occasion down the chimney.

'Can it really be the wind?' I said, 'or is it the low moan of a nun, walled up behind the chimney?'

She shivered and her eyes sparkled.

'Are there really nuns here? Were there, I mean?'

'This being an abbey, it is probable,' I said. 'Who knows what terrible rites have been enacted within these walls?'

'Henry!' said Eleanor.

But she need not have worried, Miss Morland was entranced by the idea. To be in a real abbey was a great excitement to her, and as I watched her I found myself well entertained. To be able to tease a woman is surely as important a part of love as being able to like her or respect her.

'But what is that?' I said. 'The curtain moved! What malevolent being roams outside, waiting to enter?'

Miss Morland was thrilled but said stoutly, 'It is only the wind, stirring the curtain.'

'If I could only be sure.'

'Then pray, Mr Tilney, go and look,' she said.

'I am afraid!' I said.

Eleanor laughed and said, 'I will.'

'Ah! Shamed by my sister! A slip of a girl! Then I must do the manly thing.'

And so saying I took a candle from the mantelpiece and made a show of looking behind the curtain, much to Miss Morland's delight.

'It is as you say, just the wind,' I remarked.

By the time the party broke up, it was raining violently. As the storm raged round a corner of the abbey, it closed a distant door with a bang and Miss Morland jumped. Her candle flickered, and her face was a sight to behold.

'What evil beast pursues us?' I asked.

She looked at me in awe, then caught my laughter and blushed at her own ready thoughts, but although she knew I had been teasing her, there was still a sense of expectancy about her; enough to give her a few pleasurable thrills before her first night in such an ancient building was passed.

'Do not forget that I am only two doors down from you if you should need anything,' said Eleanor to Miss Morland, as I left them to go to my own room.

Miss Morland looked grateful; for, whilst it is undoubtedly exciting to think of all the terrible things that might happen in the deep, dark reaches of the night, it is also comforting to know that help is on hand if any headless spectres should happen to creep out of the woodwork.

Saturday 23 March

A bright morning succeeded the tempest of the night, and the sun was streaming in at the windows as I sat down to breakfast at a little after eight o'clock. The ladies were not yet up and my father had already eaten so that I was alone, until Miss Morland hurried into the room; afraid, no doubt, that my father would be there, and that he would be as angry about timekeeping as he had been yesterday evening.

'Miss Morland! You are up bright and early. And how are you this morning. You slept well, I hope? No sinister apparitions disturbed you in the night? No weeping nuns or dreadful monks made their way into your room, their faces hidden by cowled habits, and dangerously flickering candles held in their blood-stained hands?'

She looked embarrassed and confessed that the wind had kept her awake.

'But we have a charming morning after it,' she added, eager to change the subject, for she was ashamed of her weakness; another thing which endeared her to me. 'Storms and sleeplessness are nothing when they are over.' Her eyes wandered out to the gardens. 'What beautiful hyacinths!' she remarked. 'I have just learnt to love a hyacinth.'

I allowed her to change the subject and we discussed flowers at length, until my father walked in. His smiling compliments announced a happy state of mind, but his hint of early rising unsettled her and evidently brought all her memories of his dislike of tardiness to mind. She murmured something about having been kept awake by the wind and therefore sleeping longer than usual, and he apologized for the weather, as though it had been his fault, and said he hoped she would not be similarly discommoded this evening. She sought for a safe topic of conversation and found it in the breakfast set. She remarked on its fineness and my father, who had chosen it, was restored to good humour.

'It is very kind of you to say so; you, who must have seen much finer things in Mrs Allen's house,' he said expansively. 'But it is neat and simple, and I have a great liking for it. Moreover, I think it right to encourage the manufacture of my own country; and for my part, to my uncritical palate, the tea is as well-flavoured from the clay of Staffordshire, as from that of Dresden or Sèvres. It is quite an old set, of course, purchased two years ago. The manufacture has much improved since that time; I have seen some beautiful specimens when last in town, and if I were not perfectly without vanity of that kind, I might have been tempted to order a new set. I trust, however, that an opportunity might ere long occur of selecting one – though not for myself.'

My father's comment took me by surprise, but I could not fail to understand it. Indeed, I think that Miss Morland was the only one at the table who did not understand him. He saw her as a bride for me! I was astonished. He had always wanted me to marry well, and the idea of him smiling on a match between me and a country miss was entirely out of character for him. I found myself wondering whether he thought the Morlands were an old family, perhaps related to some titled person, and if that was the attraction for him, not money. I put the idea to Eleanor when we were alone after breakfast, Miss Morland having left us to write to her family.

'It is possible, I suppose,' she said.

'I will endeavour to find out. I have to go to Woodston for a few days and will soon be on my way. There are sermons to be preached, parishioners to be visited and pen-wipers to be accepted. Then, too, there is parish business to discuss. The possibility of diverting the stream is as important to the people of Woodston as the battles raging on the continent are to my brother. But I mean to look into Miss Morland's ancestry. It seems clear, from everything she has said, that she is not wealthy, and so my father is either deluding himself for reasons we cannot begin to fathom, or else he thinks she will bring with her an antique pedigree that will add to our consequence in the world.'

We parted, but met again in the hall, where Miss Morland and my father were also gathered in time to see me mount my horse and set out for my parish. I caught a glimpse of Miss Morland at the window of the breakfast-room, and I smiled to think of her eyes following me as I disappeared down the drive.

The day being fine, the journey was a pleasant one and I found myself thinking of my affections and wondering if they would prosper. Would Miss Morland be descended from an old and venerable branch of a mighty family, delighting my father and allowing him to overlook her lack of fortune? Or would she be nothing more than Miss Morland of Fullerton, and would my father's interest in her wane? Would he send her away at the end of her visit with an invitation to visit again, or with nothing more than a half hearted wish for the comfort of her journey?

And I? What did I want? As I turned into the drive of the parsonage, I thought it would be brightened by her amusing fantasies, her adoration – I am only human! – and her smiling face.

I could almost hear Frederick laughing at me. *Women! Never trust them! Play with them, amuse yourself, but never let them close to the heart of you.* But the spring air was having its effect on me and I thought that nothing would please me more than Catherine – yes, Catherine! – at Woodston.

When I reached the parsonage I retired to the library and took down the peerage in order to seek for an explanation of my father's partiality for her, but I could not find any evidence that she was important enough to appeal to him. A thought flickered into my mind that he must be growing more mellow with age, but it quickly flickered out again, and wasting no more time on his quixotic behaviour I set out for the church to preach my sermon.

There were fewer coughs and colds than previously, and more

attention paid to my words of wisdom. Indeed, from the comments afterwards I was delighted to find that almost as much attention had been paid to my words of wisdom as to the new style of knot in my cravat.

Sunday 24 March

It is amazing how many things there are to be seen to here after only a week's absence: parishioners to be visited and either soothed, berated, congratulated, comforted or uplifted; plans for new stiles to be approved; gardens to be examined; matchmakers to be avoided – and sisters to be aided and abetted, for a note arrived from Morris and I have instructed one of the grooms to take it over to the abbey tomorrow, since I do not plan to return there until Tuesday and I am sure she will like it as soon as possible.

Monday 25 March

Having finished my business sooner than expected, and being, I must confess, eager to see Catherine again, I returned to the abbey this afternoon. I found that Catherine was both more foolish and more adorable than I had suspected, for when I took the back stairs to my chamber I came upon her suddenly, and she looked at me as if I were a spectre.

'Good God!' she said in horrified accents. 'How came you here? How came you up that staircase?'

Surprised, I said that it was my nearest way from the stable-yard to my own chamber, at which she blushed deeply and said no more, but she was clearly disturbed and I could not rest until I had found out why.

On enquiring how she came to such a remote part of the

house, she said that she had been to see my mother's room. I should have known at once what was in her mind, for what mother in a novel can ever have died a natural death? She must always have been dispatched by some cruel hand; either that or imprisoned in the labyrinthine caves beneath the crumbling edifice whilst being reported as dead. But I was still in a business frame of mind and I had not yet adjusted my thoughts to Northanger Abbey or to Catherine's sensibilities, and I asked in surprise if there was anything extraordinary to be seen there.

She replied quickly, 'No, nothing at all.'

She still looked pale, however, and I thought she might have become lost and not liked to admit it. I was surprised that Eleanor had left her to wander the house alone, and said so, to which she replied quickly that Eleanor had shown her over the greatest part of the house on Saturday, but that they had been prevented from visiting this part – dropping her voice – 'because your father was with us.'

Since she seemed interested in my mother's room, I remarked that it was commodious, 'Large and cheerful-looking, and the dressing-closets so well disposed! It always strikes me as the most comfortable apartment in the house,' I said, 'and I rather wonder that Eleanor should not take it for her own. She sent you to look at it, I suppose?'

'No.'

I was surprised.

'It has been your own doing entirely?' I enquired.

She said nothing.

'Eleanor, I suppose, has talked of her a great deal?' I wondered.

'Yes, a great deal. That is – no, not much, but what she did say was very interesting. Her dying so suddenly,' she said slowly, and with hesitation, 'and you – none of you being at home – and your father, I thought – perhaps had not been very fond of her.'

A light began to dawn.

'And from these circumstances, you infer perhaps the proba-
bility of some negligence' – involuntarily she shook her head – 'or
it may be – of something still less pardonable?'

She raised her eyes towards me searchingly and I was at once
amused and appalled at her terrible imaginings, as well as being
filled with an ache of tolerant tenderness for her naïveté.

'My mother's illness,' I said, 'the seizure which ended in her
death, was sudden, but the malady itself was constitutional.
Frederick and I (we were both at home) saw her repeatedly; and
from our own observation can bear witness to her having received
every possible attention which could spring from the affection of
those about her, or which her situation in life could command.'

'But your father,' said Catherine, 'was he afflicted?'

'For a time, greatly so. You have erred in supposing him not
attached to her. He loved her, I am persuaded, as well as it was
possible for him to – we have not all, you know, the same tenderness of disposition – and I will not pretend to say that while she
lived, she might not often have had much to bear, but though his
temper injured her, his judgment never did. His value of her was
sincere; and, if not permanently, he was truly afflicted by her
death.'

'I am very glad of it,' said Catherine, blushing. 'It would have
been very shocking!'

'If I understand you rightly,' I said, wondering how far her
dreadful imaginings had gone, 'you had formed a surmise of such
horror as I have hardly words to—'

Her eyes fell.

'Dear Miss Morland, consider the dreadful nature of the suspicions you have entertained,' I said more kindly. 'Remember the
country and the age in which we live. Consult your own understanding, your own sense of the probable, your own observation

of what is passing around you. Does our education prepare us for such atrocities? Do our laws connive at them? Could they be perpetrated without being known, in a country like this, where social and literary intercourse is on such a footing, where every man is surrounded by a neighbourhood of voluntary spies, and where roads and newspapers lay everything open? Dearest Miss Morland, what ideas have you been admitting?'

We had reached the end of the gallery, and although I had done my best to be gentle with her, she wept tears of shame and ran off to her own room before I could stop her.

Eleanor coming upon me then, in time to see Catherine running away, was at a loss, and I said, 'My dear Eleanor, the antiquity of the abbey, together with your account of our dear mother's death and her preserved room, have filled Catherine's head with ideas that would make Mrs Radcliffe blush! She has fancied our father a murderer, and our mother his poor, helpless victim.'

'Oh no! Oh, Henry, I am sorry for it. I am so used to the abbey myself, and so used to our mother's death, that I never thought what effect it might all have on her.'

'Should I go after her?'

'No, leave her alone for a while so that she might compose herself. It is nearly time to dress for dinner and the activity will ensure she does not brood for too long. The idea that our father might be a murderer must have been very unsettling for her. Was she really very upset?'

'She was, but not about that. She fled in shame, for I had discovered her secret fears and shown them to be absurd.'

'Then she has been shamed in her own eyes before the man she loves.'

'Loves? Do you not think you go too far, too fast?' I asked.

'Do I? I do not think so.'

'She is very young,' I said, as I gave her my arm and escorted her back to her own room where her maid awaited her.

'Younger than you, certainly, but not too young to know her own mind, nor too young to fall in love. Or to marry.'

She looked at me expectantly.

'My thoughts have been tending in that direction,' I admitted, 'but today's adventure has shown me that she needs to see more of the world before she will be able to accept my hand; or, rather, before I will feel justified in offering it to her. Whilst she still thinks it possible, nay, likely, that a retired general, a respectable man in every way, with neighbours often visiting, can murder his wife and conceal the crime, or imprison his wife and pretend she has died, then she is not old enough for marriage.'

'Then you do mean to marry her?'

I had not thought it in those words before, but found myself replying, 'Yes, I do.'

'And so Catherine, with a pretty face and her worship of you, has done what no other young lady has managed.'

'My dear Eleanor, what are you suggesting? I hope you are not suggesting that that is all I require from a wife!'

'Well, is it not?'

'No – though I will admit that those things are very attractive! But a good heart, a generous disposition, a nature so far removed from falsehood that she can scarcely credit it in her friend, an interest in the world about her and a love of family, these things are necessary.'

'Oh. I thought all you *really* wanted was a wife who loved Gothic novels!'

'I am paid for my flippancy, am I not? My chosen bride – if she will have me – loves them so much that she thinks they are real.'

'If she will have you? I think there is no doubt of that.'

'Not yet, but there is a danger in my waiting for her to see more of the world. She will see more of the men in it, too, and might find one more to her liking.'

'If she does that, then she is lacking in taste and we will think of her no more!' she said, as we walked along the corridor. 'I wonder if Papa will agree to inviting her to London when we go there after Easter. I would like her company. We could go to the galleries and the theatre, walk in the park and visit the shops. If she liked Bath, I am sure she will like London even more.'

'A good thought. When the time comes I will suggest it.'

'Papa might suggest it first.'

'Perhaps.'

'Did you find any evidence of an impressive ancestry?' she asked.

'No, none at all. I think it must be that he wants you to have a friend, and me to have a compliant wife, for I can see no other reason for it. She talks openly of her family and the Allens, of their small houses and simple ways of going on, and no one could think, from all she says, that she is anything but what she is: a charming girl from the country.'

'Then let us hope for the best, that our father is mellowing.'

'Indeed, and if he is, then there is hope for you, too.'

She sighed and shook her head.

'I would like to think so, but no, it is impossible,' she said quietly.

'How can you be so sure? Has something happened?'

'Yes, whilst you were away I had another note.'

'Ah, yes.'

'It arrived when I was showing Catherine round the abbey, and our father discovered it. He interrupted me, calling me away from Catherine angrily – and that of course contributed to her fear of him and her belief that he was capable of terrible deeds.'

'I am sorry for it. I gave the groom instructions to hand the note to no one but yourself.'

'You must not blame him, it was not his fault.'

We had reached her room, but she could see that I was curious and she explained, 'Our father was in the stables, making sure that everything was ready to receive our guests, when he saw the groom arriving from Woodston with a note in his hands, and not unnaturally thought it must be for him. But when he took it, he discovered that it was for me. There was nothing in it that anyone could not have seen but he was angry anyway and called me away from Catherine to answer it. He dictated my reply, of course, and had me say that whilst I was grateful that Mr Morris had enjoyed his stay at the abbey there was no need for further thanks and that any future letters should be addressed to my father or brother, and not to myself. Do you think I have been wrong to write to Thomas? I have, at the least, been underhand.'

'You know my feelings on that score. I think that, having found love, you should hold on to it. I was hoping our father would come round to that way of thinking eventually, but he is more stubborn than I had supposed.'

'Or more ambitious.'

'Yes, that too,' I said 'But Thomas will never accept his dismissal. He will know at once that you did not write the note; or, rather, that you wrote it at our father's dictation.'

'Yes, he will, but it will make it difficult for him to write to me in the future. It is not fair to use your grooms to deliver the notes, nor for you to risk our father's displeasure.'

'Then what do you intend to do? End the correspondence?'

'No, not that. But I do not see a way forward,' she said in dismay. She loosed her arm and stood away from me, looking into my eyes. 'Do you think Thomas and I will ever be together?'

'Yes, I am sure of it. When you are twenty-five, you know, you inherit your fortune from our mother, and if my father has not relented by then, you will be the mistress of your own fate.'

'You are right. I hope it will not come to that. I should not like to be estranged from my family.'

'And you never will be. At least not from me.'

She took my arm and gave it a grateful squeeze.

'And from Frederick?' she asked.

'No, not from Frederick either, though I suspect he will only call on you to annoy our father, instead of any nobler reason.'

'Well, if so, it is enough. He has still not forgiven our father for interfering in his life, then? You have talked with him more on the subject than I have.'

'No, he has not forgiven him and I suspect he never will,' I said. 'It hurt him too deeply.'

'Then you think Papa was wrong to send him into the library when Miss Orpington was there professing love for his friend, knowing what Frederick would find?'

'My dear Eleanor, that is a question I cannot answer. If Papa had done nothing, then Frederick might have married her before discovering her true nature, and that would have been a tragedy indeed. As it is, that tragedy was avoided, but another one unfolded. Frederick was too much in love with her to see what he saw and not be deeply hurt. If my father had waited a few weeks, a month even, then Frederick might have begun to suspect for himself, and it would not have come as such a terrible shock.'

'And the shock, being less, might have been sooner recovered from,' said Eleanor.

'But who are we to say what might or might not have happened? And anyway, what does it matter? It is done. It cannot be changed.'

'No, that is the pity of it, for it dealt Frederick a terrible blow and I cannot say that he has ever full recovered,' said Eleanor. 'I remember Frederick as he was when we were children. He was not as he is now. I wish he could go back to being like that again, for although he was always in trouble it was no more than boyish mischief, and he was never morose.'

There was time for no more. We had to dress for dinner.

'Be kind to Catherine tonight,' I said to Eleanor as we parted. 'She was very upset when she left me, ashamed of her thoughts, which cast our father in such a tyrannical light. Yes, I know he can be a tyrant, but fortunately he has not yet taken to murdering anyone!'

She smiled and promised to do everything in her power to make Catherine comfortable.

Half an hour more and I was dressed and ready to go into dinner. Catherine looked up hesitantly as I entered the room. She looked sick and pale. I took pains to set her at her ease, complimenting her dress and diverting her thoughts with an account of my time at Woodston. She smiled at my anecdotes, particularly at the story of the runaway cow, and laughed when she learnt it had tried to eat the silk flowers on Mrs Abercrombie's hat, so that by the end of the evening, her spirits were raised to a modest tranquillity.

The longer she is here, the better she will come to understand the abbey and my family, and I would very much like to take her to Woodston and show her where I live, so that she might come to know it and like it as much as I do. With a father and brother in the church she is well used to parsonages and I believe that, in time, she will come to appreciate the ease and convenience of its newly fitted state, rather than regret its lack of antiquity. Until then, the catacombs beneath the church should be able to satisfy even a lover of *Udolpho* with their dark and dreary passages. I must remember to show them to Catherine!

Wednesday 27 March

The morning being fine, I persuaded Catherine and Eleanor to walk with me. I saw that there was still some anxiety on Catherine's part, as if she feared I would raise the subject of her misunderstanding, but I scrupulously avoided any mention of anything that could have called it to mind and talked instead of Bath.

'Have you had a letter from your brother since you came to the abbey?' I asked.

'No, but I did not expect one,' she said. 'James said that he would not reply until his return to Oxford, and Mrs Allen said she would not reply until they had returned to Fullerton. But I am surprised I have not heard from Isabella.'

'Have you written to her? You know there is paper in the drawing room, with ink and pens and everything you might need? You have only to leave your letters on the table in the hall when you have finished them, and they will be taken to the post with the rest of the mail.'

She thanked me, and said that she had written to Isabella but still not received a reply.

'It really is unaccountable,' she said. 'She promised to write to me and let me know how things went on with James, and when she promises a thing, she is scrupulous in performing it, she told me so herself! I cannot think what has happened unless her letter has gone astray.'

'I have never known a letter go astray before, but it is certainly possible, and if you have Isabella's word for her faithfulness as a correspondent you can surely not need anything else,' I said.

She looked at me doubtfully but I said no more. I leave it to time and experience to teach her the value of the protestations of an Isabella Thorpe.

APRIL

Saturday 6 April

This morning brought a letter from Oxford for Catherine. Knowing how she longed for a one I was happy to hand it to her. She took it eagerly, and sat down to read it. She had not read three lines, however, before her countenance suddenly changed and she let out a cry of sorrowing wonder, showing the letter to contain unpleasant news. Watching her earnestly as she finished, I saw plainly that it had ended no better than it had begun. I was prevented from saying anything by my father's entrance and we went to breakfast directly, but Catherine could hardly eat anything. Tears filled her eyes, and even ran down her cheeks as she sat. The letter was one moment in her hand, then in her lap, and then in her pocket; and she looked as if she knew not what she did. My father, between his cocoa and his newspaper, had luckily no leisure for noticing her; but to Eleanor and myself her distress was equally visible. As soon as she could, Catherine hurried away to her own room. Eleanor half-rose to follow her, but then thought better of it and sat down again.

'I will give her a little time to compose herself,' she said, 'but then I will go to her.'

We went into the drawing room. Hardly had we begun to speculate on the nature of the news which Catherine had received when, driven from her room by the housemaids, who were making the bed, Catherine opened the door. She hesitated, having evidently sought out the drawing-room for privacy. She drew back, begging our pardon, but such was her distress that I could not bear to leave her to wander the corridors in search of a quite corner in which to give way to her feelings. I was on my feet at once, and taking her gently by the shoulders I guided her into the room and into a chair.

'If there is anything I can do to comfort you, then pray let me know,' said Eleanor tenderly, taking her hand with sympathy. 'You have had some bad news, I fear.'

But Catherine was too affected to speak.

We withdrew, to give her the privacy she needed, and retired to the breakfast-room, where she joined us half an hour later. After a short silence, Eleanor said, 'No bad news from Fullerton, I hope? Mr and Mrs Morland – your brothers and sisters – I hope they are none of them ill?'

'No, I thank you,' she said with a sigh. 'They are all very well. My letter was from my brother at Oxford.' Then speaking through her tears, she added, 'I do not think I shall ever wish for a letter again!'

'I am sorry,' I said, closing the book I had just opened. 'If I had suspected the letter of containing anything unwelcome, I should have given it with very different feelings.'

'It contained something worse than anybody could suppose! Poor James is so unhappy!'

I wondered if James was still engaged to Isabella, or if Frederick's attentions had brought about a breach. If the former, I pitied Morland, and if the latter, I was ashamed of Frederick, but whatever the case, I thought that Morland was lucky to have such a sister. I was tempted to reach out a hand to her but I had to be content with letting Eleanor comfort her instead.

'To have so kind-hearted, so affectionate a sister,' I said, 'must be a comfort to him under any distress.'

She was agitated and did not at once reply, but then she said. 'I have one favour to beg; that, if your brother should be coming here, you will give me notice of it, that I may go away.'

'Our brother! Frederick!' said Eleanor.

'Yes; I am sure I should be very sorry to leave you so soon, but something has happened that would make it very dreadful for me to be in the same house with Captain Tilney.'

Eleanor was surprised but I realized my suspicions were true and murmured, 'Miss Thorpe.'

'How quick you are!' cried Catherine, 'you have guessed it, I declare! And yet, when we talked about it in Bath, you little thought of its ending so. Isabella – no wonder now I have not heard from her – Isabella has deserted my brother, and is to marry yours!'

I frowned, for I could not believe it. He was capable of making mischief, but not, I was sure, capable of marrying an Isabella Thorpe.

I said as much, but she replied, 'It is very true, however; you shall read James's letter yourself. Stay; there is one part—'

She blushed.

'Will you take the trouble of reading to us the passages which concern my brother?' I asked.

'No, read it yourself,' cried Catherine, and blushed again. 'James only means to give me good advice.'

She handed me the letter, and I read it with a mixture of compassion and curiosity, particularly the part she seemed to find embarrassing. Her brother said that all was over between him and Miss Thorpe; that he relied upon his sister's friendship and love to sustain him; that he hoped her visit to Northanger Abbey would be over before the engagement between Isabella and Frederick was announced, so that she would not be placed in an uncomfortable position; that he had believed that Isabella loved him, because she had said so many times; and that he could not understand why she had led him on, unless it was to attract Frederick the more. But even that reason did not satisfy him, for he could not think it had been necessary, and that he wished now he had never met her, particularly as his father had kindly given his consent to the match.

The last line gave the key to her blushes, for he ended the letter by advising his sister to be careful how she gave her heart.

I was grieved for him, and grieved for Catherine. I was also grieved for Frederick, for whatever his faults, he deserved better than Isabella Thorpe.

I returned the letter, saying, 'Well, if it is to be so, I can only say that I am sorry for it. Frederick will not be the first man who has chosen a wife with less sense than his family expected. I do not envy his situation, either as a lover or a son.'

Eleanor was looking perplexed, and Catherine handed her the letter.

'My dear Catherine, I am more sorry than I can say,' said Eleanor, when she had read it. 'I can scarcely believe it. I know very little of Isabella, and so I do not know what to think. I saw her once or twice in Bath, but not to speak to, except to exchange the usual pleasantries. I find it hard to believe that Frederick intends to marry her. What are her connections? And what is her fortune? For although I think Frederick would be capable of marrying a woman without either of those things to recommend her, I believe she would have to have a number of personal qualities which Isabella, from my acquaintance with her, would seem to lack. I cannot imagine Frederick risking our father's displeasure for anything less than love, and I have seen nothing in him lately to suggest that condition.'

'Her mother is a very good sort of woman,' was Catherine's answer.

'What was her father?'

'A lawyer, I believe. They live at Putney.'

'Are they a wealthy family?'

'No, not very,' said Catherine. 'I do not believe Isabella has any fortune at all: but that will not signify in your family. Your father is so very liberal! He told me the other day that he only valued money as it allowed him to promote the happiness of his children.'

Eleanor and I glanced at each other. My father might say that nothing else mattered but unless he had changed even more than we suspected, he was very far from believing it.

'But,' said Eleanor, after a short pause, 'would it be to promote Frederick's happiness, to enable him to marry such a girl? She must be an unprincipled one, or she could not have used your brother so. And how strange an infatuation on Frederick's side! A girl who, before his eyes, is violating an engagement voluntarily entered into with another man! Is not it inconceivable, Henry? Frederick too, who always wore his heart so proudly! Who found no woman good enough to be loved!'

'That is the most unpromising circumstance, the strongest presumption against him. When I think of his past declarations, I give him up. Moreover, I have too good an opinion of Miss Thorpe's prudence to suppose that she would part with one gentleman before the other was secured. It is all over with Frederick indeed! He is a deceased man – defunct in understanding. Prepare for your sister-in-law, Eleanor, and such a sister-in-law as you must delight in! Open, candid, artless, guileless, with affections strong but simple, forming no pretensions, and knowing no disguise.'

'Such a sister-in-law, Henry, I should delight in,' said Eleanor with a smile.

'But perhaps,' observed Catherine, being so lacking in self-consequence, vanity and artifice, that she did not know what Eleanor meant, 'though she has behaved so ill by our family, she may behave better by yours. Now she has really got the man she likes, she may be constant.'

'Indeed I am afraid she will,' I replied; 'I am afraid she will be very constant, unless a baronet should come in her way; that is Frederick's only chance. I will get the Bath paper, and look over the arrivals.'

'You think it is all for ambition, then? And, upon my word, there are some things that seem very like it. I cannot forget that, when she first knew what my father would do for them, she seemed quite disappointed that it was not more. I never was so deceived in anyone's character in my life before.'

'Among all the great variety that you have known and studied,' I said, and could not resist a smile.

'My own disappointment and loss in her is very great; but, as for poor James, I suppose he will hardly ever recover,' she said sadly.

I felt for her, and thought that the best thing was to laugh her out of her melancholy. For although it was on the surface of it a misfortune, I could not help thinking that James and his sister had both had a very narrow escape.

'Your brother is certainly very much to be pitied at present; but we must not, in our concern for his sufferings, undervalue yours. You feel, I suppose, that in losing Isabella, you lose half yourself: you feel a void in your heart which nothing else can occupy. Society is becoming irksome; and as for the amusements in which you were wont to share at Bath, the very idea of them without her is abhorrent. You would not, for instance, now go to a ball for the world.' Becoming a thought more serious, and wanting to show her that what she had lost was not so very great after all, I went on, 'You feel that you have no longer any friend to whom you can speak with unreserve. No one on whose regard you can place dependence, or whose counsel, in any difficulty, you could rely on. You feel all this?'

'No,' she said, after a few moments' reflection, 'I do not. Ought I? To say the truth, though I am hurt and grieved, that I cannot still love her, that I am never to hear from her, perhaps never to see her again, I do not feel so very, very much afflicted as one might have supposed.'

Thinking enough time had been spent on such unhappy thoughts, I said, 'Come, let us explore the woods. It is still spring, whatever our relatives may be doing to upset or vex us, and the day is fine. Who knows, but we may find a hyacinth.' I turned to Eleanor. 'Catherine has but lately learned to love a hyacinth.'

'Then by all means, let us go,' said Eleanor.

Catherine became calmer throughout the walk, and jumped only twice this evening when Frederick's name was mentioned by my father, but for the rest of the evening she was tolerably comfortable, and I must hope that by the end of the week she will be able to think of it with no more than a passing sigh.

Wednesday 10 April

The subject of Isabella's engagement – supposed engagement – to Frederick has been frequently canvassed by Eleanor, Catherine and myself.

'I cannot believe that Frederick will marry someone as lacking in fortune and consequence as Isabella,' said Eleanor, as we retired to the library after breakfast, a heavy rain having set in.

'Even if Frederick was set upon such a path, which I beg leave to doubt, my father will never countenance it,' I said. 'He will certainly oppose the connection, and without his blessing it will be difficult for Frederick to marry. He has his soldier's pay, but that is little enough, and for anything more he still looks to my father.'

'But I have heard your father say, many times, that he has no interest in money,' Catherine ventured.

Eleanor and I exchanged glances. It was true that my father

frequently said as much, but did not mean it. Why, then, he said it we did not know. To make himself seem more agreeable, perhaps? But why should he want to make himself agreeable to Catherine? It plagued me. As a friend for Eleanor? Yes. But there was something more. As a possible wife for me? But she was no heiress. Was that why he said that money did not count? But why, if money did not count, had he spent so many years throwing heiresses at my head?

'You must give me warning if your brother is to come to Northanger,' said Catherine, 'for indeed, I cannot meet him.'

'You can be easy on that score, I am sure,' said Eleanor. 'Frederick will not have the courage to apply in person for our father's consent. He has never in his life been less likely to come to Northanger than at the present time.'

Catherine was somewhat mollified, but said, 'You must tell your father what sort of person Isabella is, for your brother cannot be expected to tell him everything.'

'He must tell his own story,' I said.

'But he will tell only half of it,' she protested.

'A quarter would be enough,' I returned.

'Perhaps that is why he stays away,' said Eleanor.

And indeed it seems only too likely.

This mollified Catherine and by and by, when the rain stopped, we walked into the village, where Eleanor wanted to buy some ribbon. The conversation moved on to Catherine's family and I learned more about her brothers and sisters, all nine of them, and thought what a difference it must make in the family to be ten children instead of three.

'I have two older brothers besides James,' said Catherine, 'and six younger brothers and sisters.'

'And did you spend your time nursing sick animals when you were younger?' I asked her.

She looked at me in surprise.

'No, never. I used to play cricket instead.'

'You were almost an entire team,' I said.

'With Papa, yes, we were, but of course only one team,' she said. 'We sometimes played with our neighbours but more usually we made two teams, dividing those who wanted to play into equal numbers, though it was never very equal in other ways because William is always wanting to win and Ned is always thinking about something else – he wants to be an inventor.'

'And what does he want to invent?'

'Something to hang the washing out. He is forever thinking of ways to make Mama's life easier for her, or easier for Papa.'

'If he ever invents such a marvel you must let me know,' I said. 'I am sure I will be able to persuade my father to buy such a machine for the abbey. He has every labour-saving device known and I sometimes think that that is the cause of his bad temper: he has nothing left to improve.'

'Well, if Ned manages it, I will be sure to tell you,' she said.

It emerged that she was not particularly fond of music, having learnt the spinet at eight years old and abandoned it at nine; that her sketches were confined to drawings on the backs of envelopes; that she learnt writing and accounts from her father and French from her mother, – 'but I am not very good at them,' she artlessly remarked – and that her chief delight as a child had been rolling down the hill at the back of the house.

She drew such a picture of carefree happiness that Eleanor and I were engrossed, for it was a childhood far removed from our own, and although I would like my own children to have a more organized education, I confess I would very much like to see them rolling down the hill at the back of the parsonage, to the scandal – no doubt – of the neighbourhood.

Thursday 11 April

Eleanor and I returned to the subject of Frederick's absence this morning, whilst Catherine wrote to her brother. We could not decide what Frederick was about.

'If he truly means to marry Isabella, then he must speak to my father at some point, but he does not show his face,' I said.

'I think he stays away because of his engagement,' said Eleanor. 'We know he is on leave and there is no need for him to avoid the abbey unless he wishes to avoid our father. He knows how angry Papa will be and he dare not face him.'

'Frederick has never wanted for courage, whatever else might be his failings: I have been expecting him for days. I cannot understand why he stays away. If he were truly engaged then I think he would come here at once. I think his behaviour is wholly incompatible with the supposed engagement,' I said. 'I have wondered at times whether Frederick entered into the engagement for the sole purpose of annoying our father. I have also wondered whether the engagement really exists, except in Isabella's mind. And even if it exists I wonder whether he will see it through, or will he jilt Isabella, in the way she jilted Morland?'

'Surely not?' asked Eleanor, but she did not look convinced. She was thoughtful and then shook her head. 'It is no good, no matter how much I think about it, it remains a mystery. Frederick does not even write. My father looks for a letter every morning and never finds one.'

'But Frederick has never been a good correspondent,' I remarked.

Catherine joining us at that moment, we set out for our walk. Catherine and Eleanor took their sketchpads with them and sat by the lake, as pretty a sight as anyone could wish for, and Eleanor shared her knowledge of art with her willing pupil whilst I entertained them with my conversation. We were enjoying ourselves so much that we lost track of time and were almost late for dinner. Catherine dressed quickly and was downstairs before either Eleanor or myself, a change from the first night when she amused herself by looking through old chests of linen!

Conversation at dinner was the same as always, with my father worrying that Catherine might be bored, and that the sameness of every day's society and employments would disgust her with the abbey.

'I wish the Lady Frasers were here,' he said. 'They would be good company for you. Such well-behaved, pretty girls. We might have a ball if they were here, eh, Henry? But perhaps we can have one without them. I wonder how many young people are in the neighbourhood. What do you think, Henry, Eleanor? Are there enough for a ball?'

He knew as well as I did that it would be difficult to find seven young people within ten miles at such a dead time of year, when most of our friends and neighbours were in Bath, or visiting relatives.

'But we must not neglect Miss Morland. We must show her something of the country. The next time you go to Woodston, Henry, we will take you by surprise some day or other.'

I was much taken with the idea and said, 'An excellent scheme,' and Catherine looked delighted.

'And when do you think, sir, I may look forward to this pleasure?' I asked. 'I must be at Woodston on Monday to attend the parish meeting, and shall probably be obliged to stay two or three days.'

'Well, well, we will take our chance some one of those days. There is no need to fix. You are not to put yourself at all out of your way. Whatever you may happen to have in the house will be enough. I think I can answer for the young ladies making allowance for a bachelor's table. Let me see; Monday will be a busy day with you, we will not come on Monday; and Tuesday will be a busy one with me. I expect my surveyor from Brockham with his report in the morning; and afterwards I cannot in decency fail attending the club. I really could not face my acquaintance if I stayed away now; for, as I am known to be in the country, it would be taken exceedingly amiss; and it is a rule with me, Miss Morland, never to give offence to any of my neighbours, if a small sacrifice of time and attention can prevent it. They are a set of very worthy men. They have half a buck from Northanger twice a year; and I dine with them whenever I can. Tuesday, therefore, we may say is out of the question. But on Wednesday, I think, Henry, you may expect us; and we shall be with you early, that we may have time to look about us. Two hours and three quarters will carry us to Woodston, I suppose; we shall be in the carriage by ten; so, about a quarter before one on Wednesday, you may look for us.'

The matter was settled. I withdrew at once and made preparations for my departure, then attended the ladies, booted and greatcoated.

'Our pleasures in this world are always to be paid for,' I said by way of apology, 'and because I am to have the pleasure of your company at Woodston on Wednesday, I must go away directly, two days before I intended it.'

Catherine was gratifyingly disappointed, wanting to know why that should be, and not knowing whether or not I was serious when I said that I must frighten my housekeeper out of her wits, in order to prepare for the visit.

My room in particular will need a great deal of tidying if it is to be fit to show visitors, for I must attempt to get rid of the litter of papers, the tangle of fishing lines and the hairs left by the dogs.

Catherine protested that it was not necessary and that my

father himself had said that I must not make any effort; little knowing that he expects me to arrange everything perfectly, whatever he might say.

If it were not already Saturday I might have returned in the meantime, but tomorrow is Sunday and I must not neglect my duties. Poor Langton has taken enough of my sermons these last few weeks, and I must give my parishioners the benefit of my instruction, which of course is more beneficial than Langton's instruction, since he has two fewer capes to his greatcoat and rides a horse with only three legs; or at least, travels at the pace of such a beast, which is the same thing.

I have given instructions to my housekeeper and therefore between us we hope to make the place tolerable for Wednesday's visitors.

Sunday 14 April

The weather being fine, the church was full this morning. The Miss Bridges were wearing their finest bonnets, and Miss Lowry had surpassed herself with her flowers. There was a newly stitched hassock to be admired and a new baby to be kissed. Miss Jenson had made me a pot of jam, which her mother declared to be the finest in the country, and I accepted dinner invitations for Monday and Tuesday, having no excuses ready. And so the Jensons are to have the pleasure of my company on Monday and the Viscontis on Tuesday.

Monday 15 April

The parish meeting was like all the parish meetings that have gone before and like all the parish meetings that will come after: a lot of hot air expelled by various worthy burghers on subjects as pressing as the right of way across the long meadow, the state of the path that runs beside the stream and the repair of the wall at the crossroads. The arguments raged, their proposers declaiming with the passion of the orators in the Houses of Parliament, and with glances so angry that a battleground full of generals could not have produced anything finer. But at last the matters were resolved, if not to the pleasure of all, at least to the satisfaction of some. And so the subjects will sleep until the next time they are raised and are canvassed with equal vehemence.

This evening was spent at the Jensons. Mrs Jenson remarked on the masculine nature of the parsonage and the need for a woman's softening touch, whilst the Miss Jensons sang, played and chattered cheerfully in French, all but beating me over the head with their accomplishments. But alas for the Miss Jensons! My heart is already taken, and by a young lady who neither sings nor plays nor speaks French, at least not particularly well, but who nevertheless amuses me, endears and enchants me.

Tuesday 16 April

Knowing that my father will expect to find everything ready, there was much still to do this morning, and I was not finished with the house and the grounds until well after four. There was just time for me to dress before setting out for the Viscontis.

I had thought I was safe, for the Viscontis have no daughters, but two nieces just happened to be visiting for the day – quite unconnected to my visit, as Mrs Visconti was at great pains to assure me. The two nieces sat meekly in the corner whilst Mrs Visconti spent the evening commiserating with any poor bachelor who led a lonely existence in his solitary abode, without the benefit of a pretty wife. On many occasions I changed the subject, but she defeated me each time, showing her true Latin heritage, for whatever diversions I created, I discovered that all roads led to Rome: no matter where each conversation began, it ended relentlessly at the need of an established bachelor to take a wife.

Mrs Jenson was right about one thing, however: the rectory is very much a man's domain. I have my dogs and my guns, my books and my fishing-rods, but there is a lack of anything softer. Eleanor has tried, and her prettily painted firescreen sits in the library, whilst her samplers adorn the walls, but the place would be enlivened by yards of muslin and, yes, I confess it, by Catherine sitting on the swing in the garden, her face a picture as she is transported to all the horrors of an Italian castle by Mrs Radcliffe.

I hope her adventures in the abbey have not put her off such fare, for she was very ashamed – as if it were the end of the world – when I discovered her thoughts about my father. To be sure, I was shocked at first, but on reflection I find that I like that about her. Not for me the unthinking, unfeeling woman who wears a halo of common sense and sees nothing in an abbey but an old building with inconvenient passages. Far rather would I have a young lady whose head is in the clouds, when those clouds are filled with such startling adventures.

Wednesday 17 April

I woke early, surprised at how eager I felt to show Catherine my home. I exercised the dogs and attended to business, looking at the clock more than once in an effort to make the hands turn faster, but at last my guests arrived, and exactly when they could be reasonably looked for! I hastened out to the carriage and was delighted to see Catherine's expression as she ran her eyes over the front of the parsonage, for it was easy to see how well she liked it. As the carriage rolled to a halt I handed Catherine out, taking pleasure in her touch, and the smallness of her fingers in mine. She looked up at me, smiled and blushed, and I thought she had never looked prettier. Then she petted Caesar, who gambolled around in the way only a large Newfoundland puppy can do, and laughed at the terriers as they ran around in circles. A good start!

We had scarcely gone inside, however, when my father started interrogating her on her view of the parsonage.

'It is not much, Miss Morland, not at all what you are used to, but not too bad in its way, I think?' he asked.

She, poor creature, was too overawed by his attentions to say very much, but her eyes said all that needed to be said, at least to me: that she thought it the most agreeable house in the world. But my father did not perceive her pleasure, and went on asking for compliments in the manner of a beauty desiring constant flattery. Poor Catherine!

On he went, saying it was nothing compared to Fullerton or Northanger but, considered as a mere parsonage, it was not altogether bad. By then, Catherine was luckily too much taken up with looking round the room to pay him much attention. His talk of throwing out a bow in one breath and then objecting to his own suggestion by saying he detested such things in another, passed her by.

My father did not have it all his own way, however, for just as he talked relentlessly of improvements to the rectory, so did I talk relentlessly of anything else – her journey, her activities over the last few days – until a tray of refreshments was brought in.

The tray was piled high with good things, but although I doubt if anyone has ever seen a greater range of delicacies in a country parsonage, my father apologized for them as well.

The tea over, my father led the way out of the room with Catherine on his arm, determined to show her the rest of the parsonage and eke what compliments he could from her. I was left to walk behind with Eleanor.

'I have all the pain of loving where our father disapproves, and you have all the pain of loving where he approves,' said Eleanor. 'Neither is desirable, but, of the two, I believe you are the most fortunate.'

I could not argue, but I wish he had been less eager to sing Woodston's praises, for he frightened Catherine into silence. He was determined to show her into every corner of the house, and my own room was the next to be inspected; suitably tidied, and cleaner than it had been for a long time, with no specks of mud on the floor brought in by the dogs or by one of my boots. From there we went to the drawing room, and I smiled to see how it charmed Catherine and gave her the courage to suggest that I should fit it up, 'for it is the prettiest room I ever saw; it is the prettiest room in the world!' she said.

Any other woman would have said it with a knowing smile, but Catherine thought no further than the room, not even when my father dropped hints as large as the abbey about its wanting only a lady's taste to make it complete.

'Well, if it was my house, I should never sit anywhere else,' said Catherine artlessly. 'Oh! What a sweet little cottage there is among the trees – apple trees, too!'

And at once I imagined her sitting in an apple tree, eating an apple and reading a book. The picture charmed me.

My father, who has spent the last few years wanting to pull the cottage down, was now effusive in his praise of it, saying that if Catherine approved it, it stayed – which had the effect of silencing her again; and, though pointedly applied to by my father for her choice of the prevailing colour of the paper and hangings, nothing like an opinion on the subject could be drawn from her.

I extricated her from his attentions by the simple expedient of offering her my arm, and together we strolled round the grounds. I pointed out the improvements I had made and the future improvements I intended and she was interested in all my plans. She was delighted with the gardens and the meadows, thinking them prettier than any pleasure garden she had been in before, and I found it easier and easier to think of her being their mistress.

We walked into the village, which delighted her quite as much as the parsonage, and ended with a visit to the stables, where we played with a litter of puppies just able to roll about. Our hands met as we petted the pups, and our eyes met, and although she looked away and blushed I thought she had never been happier. If we had been alone, I would have proposed to her then and there, but alas! my father intruded with some outrageous compliment and the moment was broken.

She stood up, surprised to find it was four o'clock already, and we went inside to dine. The dinner passed muster with my father, for which I was truly thankful, and although he looked at the side table for cold meat which was not there, he ate heartily and was not unduly disconcerted by the melted butter's being oiled.

At six o'clock my guests took their leave, but not before Eleanor had said to me, in an aside, 'I see that Catherine is a lover of puppies. Was there ever anything that marked her out more clearly as a heroine?'

I laughed, and thought how fortunate I had been in finding my destiny in Bath, instead of having all the inconvenience of travelling to the Pyrenees.

Thursday 18 April

I was up with the lark so that I could finish my business here and return to the abbey, where Catherine awaited me. Once there, I found that events had moved on, for Catherine had had a letter from Isabella.

'I am ashamed that I ever loved Isabella, for it was such a letter … well, you shall hear,' said she, taking it up and reading it. '"*I have had my pen in my hand to begin a letter to you almost every day since you left Bath, but have always been prevented by some silly trifle or other.*"' Catherine's face showed what she thought of such an empty protestation. '"*I am quite uneasy about your dear brother, not having heard from him since he went to Oxford; and am fearful of some misunderstanding.*" Was there ever such falsehood? "*I rejoice to say that the young man whom, of all others, I particularly abhor, has left Bath. You will know, from this description, I must mean Captain Tilney, who, as you may remember, was amazingly disposed to follow and tease me, before you went away. Afterwards he got worse, and became quite my shadow. Many girls might have been taken in, for never were such attentions; but I knew the fickle sex too well. He went away to his regiment two days ago, and I trust I shall never be plagued with him again. He is the greatest coxcomb I ever saw, and …*"'

She stopped, remembering to whom she read, blushed, and said, 'There is more of the same. And she thinks that I will try and mend things between her and James, after such treatment, and after such a letter as this. She says she will wear nothing but purple from now on, because it is James's favourite colour, but I am sure he does not care what colour any young lady should wear, only that she be good-natured and honest. She asks me to write to James on her behalf, but James shall never hear Isabella's name mentioned by me again. So much for Isabella, and for all our intimacy! She must think me an idiot, or she could not have written so; but perhaps this has served to make her character better known to me than mine is to her. I see what she has been about. She is a vain coquette, and her tricks have not answered. I do not believe she had ever any regard either for James or for me, and I wish I had never known her.'

'It will soon be as if you never had,' I reassured her.

'There is but one thing that I cannot understand,' she went on, puzzled. 'I see that she has had designs on Captain Tilney, which have not succeeded; but I do not understand what Captain Tilney has been about all this time. Why should he pay her such attentions as to make her quarrel with my brother, and then fly off himself?'

'I have very little to say for Frederick's motives, such as I believe them to have been. He has his vanities as well as Miss Thorpe, and the chief difference is, that having a stronger head, they have not yet injured himself. If the effect of his behaviour does not justify him with you, we had better not seek after the cause.'

'Then you do not suppose he ever really cared about her?' she asked.

'I am persuaded that he never did,' I said.

'And only made believe to do so for mischief's sake?'

I bowed my assent.

'Well, then, I must say that I do not like him at all, though it has turned out so well for us. As it happens, there is no great harm done, because I do not think Isabella has any heart to lose. But, suppose he had made her very much in love with him?'

'But we must first suppose Isabella to have had a heart to lose, consequently to have been a very different creature; and, in that case, she would have met with very different treatment,' I said.

She was not satisfied, but said, 'It is very right that you should stand by your brother.'

'And if you would stand by yours, you would not be much distressed by the disappointment of Miss Thorpe. But your mind is warped by an innate principle of general integrity, and therefore not accessible to the cool reasonings of family partiality, or a desire of revenge,' I said.

She laughed, for she knew that if she were a character in *The Italian* or some other such tale, she would think of nothing but revenge. Being, however, a young lady in England, she had better things to do, and was soon complimented out of further bitterness by Eleanor and myself. She resolved on not answering Isabella's letter, after which we were very comfortable.

Our talk soon reverted to our day out and she had nothing but praise for the parsonage and Woodston, and talked a great deal about her family: of her father's livings and of her brother's expectations on entering the church. She was momentarily indignant as she remembered her father's generosity in being prepared to make one of his livings over to her brother, and Isabella's scorn at such generosity, but the moment soon passed, for to encourage indignation is beyond her.

I like the sound of Catherine's family and I look forward to meeting them before very long.

Monday 22 April

After breakfast I found myself alone with my father and he told me that he had some business to attend to in London. He said that he would be setting out tomorrow and not returning to the abbey for a week. On saying that he had a mind to rent a house there for the season, I remarked that Miss Morland had never seen London and he seized on the idea at once, saying, 'Once I have managed to secure suitable lodgings, Eleanor must invite her. An excellent thought, Henry!' and was then in a good humour for the rest of the day; as was I, for Catherine will lend charm to London and I am already looking forward to seeing her there.

Tuesday 23 April

Despite our father's good humour yesterday, and despite – or rather, perhaps, because of – his excessive compliments to Catherine before he departed, it is still a relief to have the abbey to ourselves. His presence always damps our spirits but today we did exactly as we pleased and laughed as loud and long as we liked. We were entirely at ease and did not worry about anything at all, not even being five minutes late for dinner.

'This is how it will be when we are married,' I said to Eleanor, when Catherine had retired for the night. 'I am sorry for it, but there it is. My wife will not secretly resent you, as you believed when we were children. She will not slowly poison you, or lock you in the attic.'

Eleanor gave a sigh.

'We must all bear our disappointments in life, dear brother, and it seems that having a good and charming sister, who loves me as much as I love her, is destined to be one of mine.'

Friday 26 April

I believe there has never been so much laughter at the abbey. Eleanor is lighter of spirits than she has been for a long time, and, as she has persuaded Catherine to stay for some weeks more, I am looking forward to the weeks to come. The better weather is here, we are out of doors all day, and Catherine is as energetic as we could wish, matching us on every walk. And when Eleanor is tired – or says she is tired – Catherine and I walk together and talk nonsense which nevertheless amuses us both. With her I can be myself and she is fast losing most of her shyness and, with me, showing more of herself every day.

Saturday 27 April

Alas, duty calls and I am spending today and tomorrow at Woodston, attending to the duties that I have most shamefully neglected during the week. But I will be returning to the abbey on Monday and that must be my reward.

Monday 29 April

What a difference a week makes! I can scarcely believe it. How could my father do such a thing? It is only a few days ago that he was eager to take Catherine to London, and to use her so shamefully ... When I returned to the abbey and found him in the stables, giving instructions for the coach to be readied for a journey to Hereford, I was astonished.

'Ah, Henry, so you are here,' he said, looking up and seeing me. 'Pray ready yourself immediately for a journey. We are going to Lord Longtown's for a fortnight,' he said.

I was even more astounded, and asked why, at such short notice, we were to travel so far but, instead of enlightening me, he became angry and ordered me to do as he said. I, of course, told him that it was impossible as I had left my parish business in Woodston half-finished and that there was Miss Morland to be considered, too.

'Miss Morland!' he exploded, going red in the face. 'Never mention her name to me again. That deceitful, scheming, bragging—'

I was shocked at his outburst, for I had often seen him angry, but never with so little cause.

'You are never to think of her again,' he went on. 'Now pack your things at once, we are to leave after dinner.'

'An excellent time for starting a journey!' I remarked, thinking he must have run mad.

'Enough of your impertinence, I have been lenient with you for too long. I command you to be here in an hour's time, ready to go with your father – your *father*, mark you, who has the right to command you – on a long-standing engagement.'

'So long-standing that I have heard nothing of it until today,' I returned in astonishment.

'You are growing insolent,' he said, becoming ever more angry. 'It is the way with young people nowadays, I see insolence all around me.' He broke off to shout at the grooms, who scurried away from him, affrighted, to do his bidding. Then he began to shout at me again, but having my independence I took no notice of his roars and said that if he was determined to go, I would make my apologies to Miss Morland for this sudden departure and offer to escort her home.

'I have already sent her packing. She left yesterday morning on the first coach.'

I could not believe it.

'But that must mean she was forced out of the house at daybreak!' I said, appalled.

'And not a moment too soon. We have been duped, led to believe that she was an heiress, when she was nothing of the sort. A young lady of great expectations was how she represented herself, with a dowry of ten or fifteen thousand pounds, and the heir to Mr Allen's estate as well – the future heiress of Fullerton! Pah!'

'How can you have come by such a strange fancy! She never said anything of a fortune or expectations!'

'No, she was too clever for that, but I had it all from Mr Thorpe, who, being intimate with the family, knew it all. The Morlands imposed on him just as they imposed on us. James Morland was engaged to Thorpe's sister, on the understanding that he was a man of fortune, and Thorpe himself had hopes of Miss Morland. Well, he may have her now and welcome to her!'

'You surely did not place any reliance on the word of a man like Thorpe?' I asked.

'And why should I not, when he was so intimate with the family, and when the Allens were there for all to see, childless, and taking a great interest in Miss Morland.'

'So that is why you invited her to the abbey,' I said grimly. 'I wondered, but thought it impossible you should think she was rich, when everything she said and did gave the lie to such a belief. Her clothes alone should have told you as much.'

'The Morlands have deceived everyone,' said my father, lost to reason. 'The Thorpes have been cruelly used. Having pretended to be able to give his son a generous allowance on his marriage, when brought to the point, Miss Morland's father had to acknowledge himself incapable of giving the young people even a decent support. The whole family are tricksters: a necessitous family; numerous, too, almost beyond example; by no means respected in their own neighbourhood; aiming at a style of life which their fortune does not warrant; seeking to better themselves by wealthy connections; a forward, bragging, scheming race.'

'Enough!' I said, ashamed of him, and of the avarice and folly that had led to him courting Catherine, making much of her, and then turning her out of the house; proving himself, in short, to be little less a villain than she had dreamt him. 'I will not go to Hereford with you. I will not go anywhere until I know that Miss Morland is safe.'

And with that I went into the house, where Eleanor greeted me with tears, so that I could hardly comfort her.

'Oh Henry! I am glad you are home! I have had such a terrible time,' she said. 'You will never guess – our father – lost to all reason – to turn her out of doors....'

It was some minutes before I could get anything more from

her, but having persuaded her to tell me all, she gathered her thoughts, and what she said did nothing to soften the picture I had acquired of events. Quite the opposite, for it had been even worse than I supposed.

'My father returned to the abbey on Saturday night in a towering rage and told me to send Miss Morland packing at once. I tried to reason with him, but to no avail. He frightened me with his raging and at last I had to do his bidding. As you can imagine, I was a most unwilling messenger. After what had so lately passed, when I had persuaded her to remain with us for many, many weeks longer, I had to tell her that she was no longer welcome. In short, I had to tell her a tale of such obvious fabrication that I blushed to utter it: that our father had recollected a prior engagement and that she had to leave. I was made to tell her that we must leave on Monday, and that it would not be in my power to see her again. She, dear innocent, was surprised and dismayed, but showed her true worth by summoning a smile and saying that she could go on Monday very well, and that her father and mother's having no notice of it was of very little consequence, for she was sure my father would send a servant with her half the way, and then she would soon be at Salisbury, and then only nine miles from home.'

'I cannot believe it of him. To ask her to leave without giving her parents any notice of it was bad enough; to deny her even the protection of a servant was monstrous,' I said.

'She was not even allowed to stay until Monday. My father ordered the carriage for her on Sunday morning, at seven o'clock, and she was sent packing like an adventuress. What will her father and mother say! After courting her from the protection of real friends to this – almost double the distance from her home – to then drive her out of the house, without the considerations even of decent civility! The dear creature thought she must have offended our father, to be treated thus, and I could do nothing but reassure her that she had given him no just cause of offence. She was generous to the last, saying it was of no consequence.'

'No consequence?' I asked, as angry as my father, though from a very different cause. 'To be sent away with no thought given to her comfort, or the appearance of the thing? To have to travel upwards of sixty miles, nay, nearer seventy, and to be taken by post, at her age, alone, unattended!'

'She maintained her dignity whilst I was with her, but as soon as the door was closed behind me I heard her break out into weeping. I went to her the following morning and helped her to pack. I begged her to write to me, though I had no right to ask anything of her after the way she had been treated, and she promised she would let me know that she was safe at Fullerton. Even then, I was forced to use subterfuge, for you know how my father is, and how he never lets me receive letters unless he has approved the correspondence. I had to ask her to write to me under cover to my maid. Thank God I thought to ask her if she had any money, and to furnish her with what she needed for the journey, otherwise I dread to think what might have happened to her. But I think the thing that wounded her most was that she did not get to take her leave of you. She asked me very humbly to give her remembrances to you.'

I thought of her sweet nature and I shook my head in disbelief. That anyone could so use her....

'She must have passed close by Woodston as she travelled,' I said. 'I wish I had known. I would have stopped the coach and escorted her myself.'

'And now we are to see no more of her. My father has forbidden me even to think of her! And all because he imagined her an heiress, through no fault of her own. When I think of the way he encouraged her, and encouraged you to think of her, and now he has done to you what he has done to me, banished your beloved—'

'But I, at least, have my independence, and need take no notice,' I said.

'But what do you intend to do?' she asked.

'What I have intended to do for many weeks past. Ask her to marry me.'

'But our father has expressly forbidden any such thing. You would not dare cross him.'

'Indeed he would not,' came a voice from behind us. Our father had entered the room. 'Eleanor, you are not ready. The coach will leave in half an hour. If your things are not packed you will go without them.'

I nodded to Eleanor and she left the room.

'And you, sir, will do the same,' he said.

'No, I will not. I will do what I would have done anyway, before many more weeks had passed: offer Miss Morland my hand.'

'You will do no such thing!' he roared.

'You cannot stop me,' I said, looking him in the eye. 'I believe she is in love with me, and I am most certainly in love with her. Do you now expect me, having encouraged her affections, to jilt her? For I am bound to her in honour as well as in affection, as much as if there had been a formal engagement between us.'

'But there is no engagement, and once you are in Hereford and she is back in Fullerton, there will never be any suggestion of one.'

'I am not going to Hereford.'

'You will do as you are told!'

'No, sir, I will not. You cannot command me. I am my own man. You must go to Hereford without me – though why you still think it necessary to go, since it was an excuse trumped up at a moment's notice, to rid yourself dishonourably of Miss Morland, I cannot imagine. And I am going to Fullerton.'

'Why, you—'

I left him blustering, and we parted in dreadful disagreement. I was in such an agitation of mind that I returned almost instantly to Woodston to compose myself. But tomorrow I go to Fullerton.

Tuesday 30 April

I am now over half-way to my destination. Tomorrow my fate will be decided. Will Catherine forgive me for my father's behaviour? What will her family think? Will her father allow me to pay my addresses to her, after the way she was shamefully used? I can only hope so.

MAY

Wednesday 1 May

This morning found me at Fullerton, a village not unlike Woodston, where I looked about me and saw, at some small distance, the church, and beside it the parsonage. As I made my way to the gate I found myself the object of every eye, for travellers were evidently little seen in the neighbourhood. As I approached the house I found that I was observed by a collection of children, Catherine's brothers and sisters, who had gathered at the window on hearing the telltale sounds of a visitor. I rang the bell and was admitted to the drawing room, where I found Catherine alone. She sprang up and said, startled, 'Henry!'

And with that one word I knew she was mine.

She blushed and stammered and offered me a seat, which I took, but hardly had I sat down when her mother entered the room, closely followed by sundry brothers and sisters.

I sprang up and Catherine introduced me.

'I must apologize for my sudden appearance. I have no right to expect a welcome here after what has passed, but I had to be sure that Miss Morland had reached her home in safety. I knew nothing of her sudden departure, being attending to business in my own parish, and I am more sorry than I can say that she was left to endure such a journey alone,' I immediately began.

Mrs Morland was generous in her reception of me, saying, 'Well, now, if that is not good of you, Mr Tilney. I am sure it was not your fault that Catherine had such a strange journey and there is no harm done, as you see. Besides, it is a great comfort to find that Catherine is not a poor helpless creature, but can shift very well for herself.'

I began to apologize for my father but she did me the kindness of judging me apart from him and saying that she had long been wanting to thank me for my friendship towards Catherine.

'She has told us a great deal about you and your sister in her letters. We are always happy to see Catherine's friends here. The future is what matters, and the present, not the past. Pray, do not say another word about it.'

I was not ill–inclined to obey her request, for, although my heart was greatly relieved by such unlooked–for mildness, it was not in my power to say anything at all. Seeing Catherine again, having so much to say to her that could not be said in company, rendered me mute and I sat down again in silence.

Mrs Morland sent one of the younger children for Mr Morland, feeling, no doubt, that he would introduce a new topic of conversation. Whilst we waited, she asked about the weather, my journey, and a dozen other such commonplaces. I made the usual replies whilst watching Catherine, who looked anxious, agitated, happy and feverish. She guessed, of course, why I had called. If I had been merely solicitous over her safety I could have written her a letter. A visit spoke of something more.

At length, no more remarks about the state of the roads and the mildness of the day for the time of year could be made, and we awaited Mr Morland in silence, only to learn some minutes later that he was from home. When the conversation dwindled to nothing I roused myself and asked after the Allens, then saying that I wished to pay them my respects I asked Catherine if she would show me the way.

'You may see the house from this window, sir,' said her sister Sarah helpfully.

Her mother silenced her with a nod and Catherine and I set out.

'Miss Morland ... Catherine,' I said, as soon as we had turned out of the drive. 'I have that to say to you which ... I think you can guess ... that is to say ... Catherine, I think you know what my feelings are for you.'

She blushed and said, 'You like me as the friend of your sister.'

I took her hand, which relaxed in mine as she felt the touch of my fingers, for I had removed my gloves on entering the house and neglected to put them on again, whilst she had forgotten hers.

'As more than that,' I said. 'Much more. I thought I would have plenty of time to say this ... I thought you were to stay at the abbey for several weeks more ... but now I can wait no longer. You have my friendship, my love, my affection, my heart. Tell me, Catherine, do I have yours?'

She looked down, and murmured, 'You do,' so quietly that I had difficulty hearing it.

I smiled.

'I know you like my parsonage and I think you like me. If I promise to fit up the drawing room in the way you like, will you come and live there with me? Will you be my wife?'

Her reply was everything I could have wished for. To be sure, she was incoherent, and her sense of obligation and pleasure were so mixed together with an assurance that her heart had long been my own that her words were incomprehensible, but the smile in her eyes told me all I needed to know.

I took advantage of the quietness of the lane to kiss her.

We were disturbed by the clop of hoofs and sprang apart before the horseman turned the corner, then smiled and laughed. I gave her my arm and we walked on together, with the sun shining far more splendidly than usual and the bees buzzing lazily and the birds chirruping in more than usually good voice.

As we turned into the lane I knew I must give her an account of my father's behaviour and although I was ashamed to do it, I told her all. She was startled to find that he had thought her an heiress, but not at all surprised that the mistake had been caused by John Thorpe, whose family had caused hers such distress.

'So that is why I was invited to Northanger Abbey,' she said.

'By my father, yes, but not by Eleanor or myself. We wondered why he was making so much of you, but as we knew you to be poor we thought he was being kind to Eleanor at last and securing for her the cheerful company of a valued friend.'

I told her that it was Thorpe again who, on seeing my father in London, and being angry because Catherine's brother refused to have anything more to do with Isabella, had claimed that Catherine had deliberately lied about her fortune in order to mislead everyone.

'Though how my father could have believed it, when he knew you and knew you to be incapable of such deceit, I cannot imagine. His anger was not really at you, but at himself for being so easily duped.'

'And the visit to Hereford?' she asked.

'I am ashamed to say there had been no prior engagement, he simply arranged to leave the abbey at once so that he could request you to leave – nay, throw you out of the house. I thought your suspicions of him foolish when you first arrived at the abbey, but you were not so far wrong in your estimation of him: in driving you out of the Abbey at a moment's notice he behaved like a veritable Marquis or Montoni.'

A few minutes more brought us to the Allens' door, where we knocked and were admitted, to find the Allens at home. I said very little to any purpose, and Catherine said nothing at all, but the Allens I hope will forgive us when they know all.

We strolled back to the parsonage through the spring sunshine and I had to tell her that my father had forbidden me to think of her ever again, whereupon she said she was glad she had not known of his disapproval before I had proposed, otherwise she might have felt compelled to refuse.

'Then it is a good thing I forgot to mention it,' I said.

She smiled, and we finished our walk in perfect happiness.

Such happiness cannot last, and when we returned to the house it was to find that Catherine's father had returned also, and that he was in the sitting room with her mother. The younger children being outside I made the most of the moment and, leaving Catherine to wander the garden, I asked to speak to them.

Their surprise on being applied to for their consent to my marrying Catherine was, for a few minutes, considerable.

'It never entered our heads there might be an attachment,' said Mr Morland, and I could see that it was so. 'She never said anything of it.'

'But was very downcast when she returned home, and now I know why,' said Mrs Morland. 'I thought it was on account of leaving her fine way of living behind. Now I know it was something far more to her credit; on account of leaving loved ones.'

'I should not wonder at it,' said Mr Morland. 'There is nothing more natural than Catherine being loved. We love her very much ourselves.'

'Then I may have your consent?' I asked.

'Aye, and gladly. Mr and Mrs Allen speak well of you, and you seem just the sort of young man to make Catherine happy.'

'She will make a sad, heedless young housekeeper to be sure,' said Mrs Morland, 'but there is nothing like practice for curing any deficiencies.'

'Luckily I have an independent fortune as well as my living, and Catherine will not need to learn economy. But there is something I should mention,' I said, for it was impossible to conceal it; and indeed I would not conceal something of such importance. 'Although I am of independent means, and I have a home to offer Catherine, my father is set against the match.'

They were troubled at that.

'How set against it?' asked Mr Morland.

'He has forbidden it.'

'Well, that is set against it indeed!' said Mr Morland.

'That is bad. That is very bad. But what can he have against our Catherine?' asked Mrs Morland.

'Nothing at all, save that he wished me to marry an heiress,' I explained.

'Well, that must be changed before you can marry,' said Mrs Morland, to my dismay. 'I will not send Catherine into a family where she is not welcome, for it will only make her unhappy. Will he come round, do you think?'

'I hope so,' I said.

'We must all hope so, for whilst your father expressly forbids the connection, we cannot allow ourselves to encourage it,' said Mr Morland. 'There must be his consent, or else how is Catherine to be happy if he will not recognize her?'

I could say no more, and so I thanked them for hearing me and went outside, where I found Catherine, and made her acquainted with everything her parents had said.

'I am sure my father will come round eventually,' I said. 'He cannot fail to love you, once the first shock has passed.'

'And if he does?'

'Then I will have to carry you off in a chaise and four, for I mean to marry you, with or without our parents' approval.'

Friday 3 May

Catherine has promised to write to me, and only that makes it tolerable for me to return to Woodston, where I must tend my plantations, preach my sermons and work upon my father until he gives his consent to the match.

Monday 6 May

At home again, and already writing to Catherine. Eleanor is delighted for me, and we commiserate with each other on our father's nature, which is keeping us both from happiness. Though my case seems the more hopeful of the two, I fear that neither Eleanor nor I will be happy very soon.

Wednesday 15 May

Although my father has banned me from Northanger, and although I am resolved never to spend a night beneath his roof, I nevertheless drove over there today to attempt to reason with him once again. I found him in the stables but when I tried to speak to him he would only roar, 'If I cannot prevent it, I will not condone it. You will not taint the abbey with such a one as Miss …' He ended in a splutter as he could not even bring himself to say her name.

'She will not live here, but at Woodston,' I said.

'And if your brother dies, what then? Am I to leave all this ...' his arm swept wide '... to a penniless girl with an enormous family of needy mouths to feed? To have the name of Tilney defiled by such a creature?'

I mastered my temper and explained that Catherine's family were neither needy nor so very numerous as he supposed, but he would not listen, and repeating that I was no longer welcome at the abbey, he mounted his horse and very nearly rode me down as he galloped from the stable yard.

Eleanor was my consolation. As I walked with her, I said, 'How do you bear it? You may come and live with me at Woodston any time, you know.'

'It is not so bad,' she said. 'Now that Margaret and Charles have returned to the neighbourhood I have more opportunities to escape, at least for a while, and the Lady Frasers are here again. You know how much our father has always liked titles and he encourages me to visit them, as well as to invite them here. And I have Catherine's and Thomas's letters.'

'What we need is a *deus ex machine*,' I said to her. 'If this were a play, then a platform would lower itself from the heavens and the gods would step forth and solve our problems with a wave of their hands. Some unforeseen and unexpected conclusion would present itself to speed a happy ending.'

She smiled, and said, 'I dread to think what Papa would say if one of the gods descended from the heavens and landed here.'

'He would probably take Zeus by the hand and lead him round the kitchen garden, pointing out the improvements he has made,' I remarked.

She gave a wry smile and said, 'Alas, such things only happen in novels.'

We were interrupted at that moment by Alice, my sister's maid, who looked about her furtively then said, 'A letter for you, miss.'

Thinking it must be from Catherine, I drew closer, but on seeing the first few words I realized it was not from Catherine at all.

'So Alice now brings you Thomas's notes as well?'

'After our father intercepted his second note, it seemed the only way.'

I wandered away to let her read it in private, but after only a minute she called me back in great excitement, smiling and then bursting into laughter.

'Oh, Henry!' she said, and then, laughing too much to speak, she handed me the letter. I took it, mystified, and read:

My Dearest, Darling Eleanor,

I am on my way to Northanger Abbey and I hope to reach you just after this letter, if not before. Something wonderful has happened, though of course it is terrible as well, and I am not at all pleased, but sadly grieved. Only you will not believe it, my uncle and cousins are all dead, killed in a freak accident! They were staying at their castle in Spain, for you know my uncle has property everywhere. The four of them were out hunting sweet, fluffy animals at the time – for they were evil men and could never limit themselves to shooting things only for food – when a storm blew up, and they were all of them struck by lightning. According to the peasant who witnessed the whole, the lightning jumped from one to another of them, so that the same bolt finished them all. So now I am a Viscount and the proud possessor of a house in town, a house in Bath, a vast country estate and of course a castle in Spain. I am fabulously wealthy, so wealthy that I cannot begin to count my fortune, but I can tell you that I have an income of a clear thirty thousand pounds a year. Dear Eleanor, you who loved me before I inherited my riches, you who are my own dear heart, say you will make me the happiest of men. I have written

to your father, explaining the change in my circumstances and
telling him I will wait upon him on Wednesday.
Your own
Thomas

I laughed along with my sister.

'My dear Eleanor, you will be the happiest of women, and there is no one who deserves it more,' I said.

'I wonder what my father will say?'

We looked at each other and laughed, wondering how he would manage such a *volte face*.

'But stay,' I said, as I handed the letter back to her. 'It says he will be here on Wednesday. That is today. The letter must have been delayed.'

Eleanor looked at me, then at Alice, then said, 'Quickly! I must change my dress!'

She had hardly reached the front door, however, when my father, newly returned from his ride, emerged, beaming all over his face.

'Do you remember that delightful young man who joined us at the abbey some years ago, a friend of Frederick's, Mr Morris?' he asked Eleanor. 'But of course you do. I felt sure you liked him, and he you. I believe he wrote to you once or twice, I remember intercepting his letters. It was quite wrong of him to write to you, of course, but it was evident he liked you and I admired him for it. It showed a pleasing spirit and a great intelligence in recognizing your worth. I happened to hear that he would be in the neighbourhood and it is possible he might call. You had better see to your dress, it will not do to have him finding you like this. Put on that new gown you had last month, I am sure he will like it.'

'This is very sudden, sir,' I could not resist saying. 'I thought you did not like Mr Morris.'

'Nonsense, I have always thought him a very fine young man, he is just the sort of young man I would like to have in the family.'

'But he has no fortune,' I said.

'What does fortune matter?' asked my father blithely. 'It matters not at all.'

'I am glad to hear you say so,' I returned. 'Then you can have no objection to Miss Morland.'

He was momentarily disconcerted, but returned with, 'Miss Morland is too young for marriage.'

'A problem that time will heal,' I said.

He waved it away.

'There is not time to think of Miss Morland now. You would not want to spoil your sister's happiness, nor take anything away from her, I am sure. Eleanor, go and dress, my dear, I think I hear a carriage.'

Eleanor, hearing it too, flew inside.

I, content to see Eleanor happy, and knowing I had at least reminded my father of Catherine and my determination to marry her, went out with him to the carriage: I wanted to give Thomas a welcome as genuine as my father's would be false. My father, in his excess of good humour, forgot that he had banished me and even smiled at me as the carriage rolled to a halt.

The door opened and Thomas stepped out. My father was at his most genial, welcoming him to the abbey and asking after his journey.

Thomas – or the viscount, as I must get used to calling him – was still dressed in his old clothes, having stopped for nothing in his eagerness to see Eleanor again. He greeted me heartily and he endured all my father's obsequiousness, although he looked momentarily put out when my father declared that no letter had arrived to prepare him for the visit. He glanced at me and, seeing my face, knew that the letter had arrived.

Disdaining to call my father a liar, he said, 'A pity. You must think it very strange of me to call, but I have a matter of great importance I would like to discuss with you. I wonder if you would favour me with a few minutes of your time?'

'But of course. My time is always at your disposal.'

And smiling benignly, he led Thomas into his study.

The outcome was never in doubt. In a few minutes Thomas emerged and, catching sight of Eleanor, who had just come downstairs, he ran to her and claimed her as his own.

I retreated to give them their privacy and thought, Now if only some similar miracle could happen for me.

JUNE

Monday 3 June

My father's complaisance towards me did not last long, and as his last words to me when I left the abbey were that he had not forgiven me for my disobedience and that I was not welcome at the abbey until I had renounced Catherine, I have not been there since. Eleanor and I now rely on letters and meetings at neighbours' houses. It was in a letter, arrived this morning, that I learnt more about the wedding plans: that our father is torn between encouraging Eleanor and Thomas to procure a special licence, so that they might marry without delay, and encouraging them to wait so that there is time for him to arrange the most splendid wedding the country has seen. He has already invited the Marquis of Longtown and General Courteney, and never tires of talking of 'my daughter Eleanor, the future viscountess.'

To remove Eleanor from his effusions I wrote back and suggested a week in London, so that Eleanor could buy her wedding clothes. I am sure she will like the idea, and now she only needs to persuade our father to let her go.

Tuesday 4 June

Our father was so taken with the idea of Eleanor's wedding clothes coming from London that he wrote to Mrs Hughes himself and begged her chaperonage.

'I am indebted to you for your kindness, Henry,' said Eleanor, as we met this afternoon at the Lady Frasers' house, 'especially as Thomas has to be in London to deal with the marriage settlements. I suppose your suggestion had nothing to do with the fact that Catherine is also to be in London soon?'

'Nothing at all,' I said airily. 'It is a complete coincidence that she is going to London next week with the Allens. If we should happen to see her about town it will be nothing but a fortunate chance.'

'And is our invitation to the Allens for dinner on Thursday a result of the same chance?'

'My dear sister, do you really want to know? Because if not, I suggest you do not ask.'

'Keep your secrets then,' she said. 'But you might wish to know that I have invited Catherine to ride with me in the park on Friday. Would you care to join me?'

'I am always happy to accompany you, dear sister,' I said.

She laughed.

'Very well, we are meeting her at ten o'clock. I must give you warning that I mean to ask her to support me when I marry. She has been a true friend to me and I hope she will carry my bouquet.'

'Our father will never allow it!' I said, startled.

'My dear Henry, he is so delighted with me that he would indulge me in any whim. Besides, I do not mean to ask him. I mean to tell him. Thomas and I are of one mind on this, that our father must be brought to sanction your marriage. I can think of no better wife for you, and no better sister for myself, than Catherine. Once Thomas and I are married you will both come and stay with us and my father will become gradually used to the idea – or, at least, he must pretend to become used to the idea if he wishes to be a guest in our house.'

'He would not sacrifice that pleasure for anything in the world.'

'And so I predict, dear brother, that there will be another wedding before the year is out.'

I thought of it with a great deal of satisfaction, and I believe I scarcely heard one word in ten that Eleanor said, for although I love my sister and I was happy to indulge her in a conversation about Thomas, I love Catherine more. Whilst Eleanor expounded on her betrothed's many virtues, I thought of the many virtues, habits and endearing quirks of my own betrothed.

Tuesday 11 June

Arriving in London, I went at once to the Allens to pay my respects. Catherine was there, as I knew she would be, and after the first ten minutes or so, Mrs Allen suggested that Catherine should show me the garden.

'It is nothing to a country garden, merely a small patch of ground, but the roses are very pretty,' said Mrs Allen.

Catherine agreed with alacrity and we were soon out of doors, walking arm in arm. We talked of Eleanor's good fortune and of her plan to reconcile my father to our own marriage.

'I am looking forward to seeing her again on Friday,' she said.

'And she you.'

'And will you be there?' Catherine asked.

'My dear Catherine, a mountain full of *banditti* could not keep me away. And after our walk, perhaps you will be good enough to accompany us to Grafton House. Eleanor needs to buy some fabric for her wedding clothes.'

'Oh, yes, and I must have something for a new dress, too. I have never been an attendant before. You must help me choose my muslin!' she said.

'Ah, you have remembered that I am an expert. Good. I will find you such a fabric as has never been seen before; a muslin so fine that countesses will exclaim at it in astonishment and yet so sturdy that even the most heavy-handed washerwoman cannot damage it on washing day; the kind of muslin that women can usually only dream of!'

'And do your really think your father will be reconciled to the match?' she asked.

'He must be, since he has no choice in the matter and can only delay and not prevent it.'

She was satisfied, and we wandered through the garden for far longer than its small size deserved, though Mrs Allen was too good to comment on the fact.

A delightful day, and a summer with Catherine to look forward to. What more could any man want?

Thursday 13 June

Mrs Hughes and Eleanor accompanied me to the Allens tonight and they all enjoyed renewing their acquaintance. They had much to talk of, Eleanor's wedding taking up most of the evening, which left Catherine and myself free to draw into a corner after dinner and talk of our own affairs.

Friday 14 June

A walk in the park and afterwards Grafton House. It was amusing to see Catherine's face, which was much as Aladdin's face must have been when he first walked into the cave. Fullerton, and even Bath, do not have shops like London! Catherine picked out a charming sprigged muslin which will make her look altogether delightful and I am all eagerness for Eleanor's wedding, which has now been arranged for the end of July.

Monday 24 June

Alas, the Allens have left London and we ourselves return to the country tomorrow. However, I have been invited to call upon them at Fullerton whenever I am in the neighbourhood, and I think I will have business there frequently over the summer!

JULY

———⚬⚬⚬———

Wednesday 17 July

Eleanor's wedding day draws on apace and yet she has still not told my father that Catherine will be her maid.

'You cannot leave it any longer,' I said to her this morning, when we met at Charles and Margaret's house.

'I know, but I am waiting for Frederick to be home,' she said.

'How so?'

'Because our father will inevitably be angry with Fredrick about something before the week is out, and that will divert his attention from my sins,' said Eleanor.

I could tell, despite her half-smile, that she was worried about telling him and I offered to do it myself.

'No, there is no need, I have made up my mind to tell him on Friday,' she said. 'Frederick's coming home tomorrow means that there will surely be something he has done to upset our father by the day afterwards.'

Charles, overhearing our conversation, said that Frederick would be sure to do something to upset our father within an hour of arriving at the abbey, never mind a day.

'And if not,' he said, as we went in to dinner, 'send me a note, Eleanor, and I will do something to annoy him myself!'

Charles's house was such a happy one that we were loath to leave. Though the building itself is in need of some repair and the kitchens are antiquated, the atmosphere is infectious. Eleanor was at her liveliest. I sometimes forget how lively she can be, how bright and sparkling, because the abbey crushes all the life from her and she is seldom anywhere else. I am looking forward to seeing her in her own home, where there will be nothing to crush her and everything to support her spirits.

When I returned to the parsonage I looked around it and made a note of the decorations I still need to complete before it will be fit to receive Catherine, for although I believe she could be happy anywhere, I want her to have a home she can be proud of.

Friday 19 July

A letter from Eleanor. She broke the news to my father and was alarmed at his anger, but upon her saying that the viscount approved of her choice, my father's rage disappeared like a summer storm. His brow smoothed and his face was wreathed in smiles.

I have found the magic words, she wrote. *Whenever he is angry I have only to say 'the viscount' and he is instantly in a good humour. Which is lucky, because Frederick has done nothing to anger him so far. And speaking of Frederick, Henry, I mean to invite him to stay with us after our marriage, and you and Catherine must come too. We will hold a house party. If Catherine and Frederick are to be related – and they are – they must put their differences behind them.*

I applaud her spirit, but I fear it will not be so simple a thing to bring about. Catherine has still not forgiven Frederick for causing her brother so much unhappiness. She talks often of her family and she loves her brothers and sisters as much as I love Eleanor. It seems that James is still unhappy, and although I believe he does not regret Isabella, it has shaken his confidence in women and he avoids their company. It will not be an easy thing for Catherine to forgive.

Friday 26 July

Eleanor's wedding day, and she has never looked more beautiful, but I am ashamed to say that I had eyes for no one but Catherine. She has become much more confident in the last few months, and although in one way it made me glad, it made me sad also, for there was something about her old naivety that I used to love. But just when I was thinking it had gone for ever, and was mourning its passing, she began to talk to me about her latest novel. Her eyes were wide and before long we were speaking of villains and dungeons just as breathlessly as before. She might no longer expect to find such adventures in England, but I am delighted to learn that she still believes such extraordinary people and amazing occurrences might exist on the

Continent, and as the war makes travel impossible, I hope she will believe so for ever.

AUGUST

Thursday 22 August

Eleanor has been true to her word and she has invited us all to a house party at her splendid new home. Our father never tires of hailing her as 'Your Ladyship' and I believe he loves her now ten times more than when she was simply Miss Tilney. Thomas is truly deserving of her and he has made her very happy.

Eleanor, Thomas, Catherine and I walked through the grounds this morning and as we went down to the lake, Eleanor and Thomas were reminiscing over their first meeting.

'I felt very awkward,' said Thomas. 'I knew so very few people and it was a relief to me to meet you' – turning to Eleanor – 'and find a kindred spirit. My poor servant was just as much overawed as I was, and the poor man was so flustered by all the grandeur of the abbey that he left behind a collection of washing bills in a cabinet. He only told me about it after we had arrived back at my modest rooms, when it was too late to reclaim them.'

Catherine started and blushed, then burst out laughing. We looked at her enquiringly, and she, torn between embarrassment and humour, revealed that she had found them late at night, but that her candle had been extinguished before she could examine them.

'You need say no more!' I exclaimed. 'You were certain you had found a letter from Matilda, telling of her cruel treatment and unnatural imprisonment by her monstrous father – or uncle – or guardian – who was determined to force her into a distasteful marriage in pursuit of his own ambitions.'

She blushed again but admitted it was so, and we all laughed together.

'I am glad they gave you such an adventure,' said Thomas. 'At least you had entertaining company from the start of your visit. When I arrived at the abbey I knew no one but Frederick.'

At the mention of Frederick, Catherine stiffened. Eleanor, seizing the moment, said, 'My brother will be joining us tomorrow.'

'Then you must excuse me if I withdraw,' said Catherine.

'But I will not excuse you,' said Eleanor. 'You must make your peace with Frederick. You are to be brother and sister, after all.'

Catherine did not like the notion but in deference to Eleanor's wishes she determined to remain and to act with at least the appearance of civility.

I wonder what tomorrow will bring.

Friday 23 August

A surprising day. Frederick arrived this afternoon and although he did no more than bow to Catherine, he watched her throughout dinner and seated himself next to her when we retired to the drawing room afterwards.

Catherine tried to excuse herself, but he would not let her go.

'You do not want to talk to me, I see, but I must insist, even though you are still angry with me for having come between your brother and his betrothed,' said Frederick.

Catherine did not deny it.

'You must have liked Isabella a great deal,' he said.

'I certainly did not,' returned Catherine. 'I never was more deceived in anyone in my life.'

'But you thought she was good enough for your brother?'

'No,' said Catherine decidedly.

'Then we have more in common than you suppose, for I did not think she was good enough for him, either.'

Catherine was surprised and then thoughtful. She said, with a frown, 'Do you mean that you came between them deliberately, because you did not want them to marry, knowing they would be unhappy?'

'Let us just say, I gave Isabella an opportunity to show her true worth and she availed herself of it,' he said. 'I felt it better that your brother should discover her true nature before he married her, rather than afterwards.'

'To be sure, that would have been very dreadful,' Catherine acknowledged.

'You are angry with me at the moment, but do you think that one day we might be friends?'

'I do not know,' she said uncertainly. 'My brother is still very distrustful of women, and you brought that distrust about. Perhaps your motives were good, but your way of going about things was not so fortunate.'

Frederick shrugged and said, 'It is the way of the world. Women are not to be trusted, and the sooner a man learns it, the better.'

'You are very severe on us,' said Margaret, who had overheard him because of a lull in her own conversation.

'Present company excepted, of course,' said Frederick. 'But I believe the only three women worth knowing are all in this room and are all, alas, either married or betrothed.'

'Oh, there are other women worth knowing,' said Charles. 'Penelope Maple, for one.'

'Pen is engaged to Lord Larchdean,' said Frederick. 'It is true, he is twenty years older than she and possesses a voice like a foghorn, but he is very rich and of course he has a title.'

'It is a very good match for her,' said my father, who had taken little interest in the rest of the conversation but who was at once alert at the mention of a lord.

Frederick gave him a look which was at once hostile and understanding.

Later, when everyone else had retired for the night, Fredrick put a hand on my arm.

'Stay,' he said. 'We have not had a chance to talk since I arrived.'

I saw that he needed to speak to someone and so I indulged him.

'I have been angry with our father for a long time, but today, talking to Catherine, I realized that I had done to her brother exactly what our father did to me, and yet I had never seen it before. I had thought our father motivated by pride and greed—'

'Which he was,' I said.

He acknowledged it.

'And yet his actions, if not his motives, were the same as mine when I flirted with Isabella Thorpe. He wanted to save me from a bad marriage and I wanted to save James Morland from the same.'

'Are you saying that you forgive our father?'

He shook his head slowly.

'No, not forgive, but perhaps – understand.'

'And have you forgiven women yet, for having betrayed you. Have you understood that not all women are the same?'

'As to that, I know they are not all the same, but unfortunately the ones that interest me are all the same. I do not have the good fortune to be attracted to a Margaret, or an Eleanor or a Catherine.'

'Or a Penelope?'

'Pen is the same as all the rest, marrying for a fortune and a title. She always said she would marry a lord.'

'And how old was she when she said it?'

'Fourteen. I remember the day distinctly. It was the day I began to lose all faith in women.'

'And are your ideas what they were at fourteen?' I asked him.

He gave a bitter laugh.

'No, for then I liked the idea of chasing women. I did not know that they were not worth catching,' he remarked.

'Then if your ideas have changed since you were fourteen, do you not think it possible that Pen has changed as well?'

'As she is to marry Larchdean, it is clear that she has stayed the same,' he said bitterly.

'I think not. I happen to know that Larchdean proposed but was turned down.'

He looked surprised, and an unmistakeable gleam crept into his eye.

'Are you sure?' he asked.

'I had it from Larchdean himself.'

He shrugged, trying to pretend he did not care, but I would not be surprised if he is called away tomorrow. It would be a strange thing if this year saw all three of us married!

Saturday 31 August

My father has done his best to ignore Catherine and the Allens, but a combination of his delight at Eleanor's marriage and my own determination have brought about a softening of his opposition. Then, too, he has discovered that Catherine's family are not so poor as he supposed. He has also discovered that the Allens, being childless, have not decided where to leave their property, and so he speculates that they might leave it to Catherine, and so at last he has withdrawn his opposition to our marriage. He has not gone so far as to give us his blessing, but he said to Eleanor this morning that I could be a fool if I liked it. And as I do like it, our marriage will shortly go ahead.

Thanks to Eleanor's intervention, I am now welcome once more at Northanger Abbey, and I intend to return there on Monday with my father, whilst Catherine will leave for Fullerton. But before long I will be with her again, for I mean to drive over to see her parents as soon as the necessary preparations have been put in hand – and before my father can change his mind!

SEPTEMBER

Monday 2 September

Frederick was waiting for us on our return to the abbey and informed us that he is newly engaged to Penelope. Since she comes of a good family and has a considerable dowry my father is pleased, and since I have heard from Frederick's own lips that he loves her, I am also pleased. And Frederick was good enough to say he was delighted to hear of the happy conclusion to my own affairs.

Tuesday 3 September

My father wrote a long and courteous letter to the Morlands, full of empty professions and meaningless phrases, which he instructed me to give to them when I next go to Fullerton. He was somewhat startled when I informed him that I intended to set out at once, but he waved me away with something like cordiality. I arrived this evening and was welcomed warmly by Mr and Mrs

Morland, who are almost as happy as Catherine and myself that our marriage can now take place.

Catherine and I have decided on an October wedding and we are to follow it with a tour of Scotland, where there are plenty of castles and mountains and dungeons to exercise her imagination. Who knows, we might be captured by *banditti* after all!

OCTOBER

Friday 11 October

After all our trials and tribulations, nothing occurred to prevent our wedding and Catherine and I were married this morning. The bells rang and everybody smiled. The perfect happy ending!